ZODIAC

NEVER LOVE A LIBRA

by Vicki Kamida

Random House Sprinters
Random House • New York

A RANDOM HOUSE SPRINTER™ PUBLISHED BY RANDOM HOUSE, INC.

Text copyright © 1995 by Vicki Kamida
Cover art copyright © 1995 by Bill Schmidt

Library of Congress Catalog Card Number: 95-70042
ISBN: 0-679-87308-2
RL: 6.5–7.0
First Sprinter edition: December 1995

Manufactured in the United States of America

10 9 8 7 6 5 4 3 2 1

ZODIAC CHILLERS is a trademark of Random House, Inc.

PROLOGUE

For him, it was love at first sight.

The girl stood at the rail of the elegant white cruise ship, her long red hair blowing off her shoulders in the soft Fort Lauderdale breeze. When she closed her eyes, tilting her head to the sun to take in the warm rays, his heart started to race.

Perfect.

He stared at her for a long time. He memorized each one of her gestures—how she twisted her hair into a knot and put it up. How she arched her neck and stretched afterward.

And all these gestures told him he wanted to know everything there was about her. And more.

I don't know who you are, he thought, *but you can be sure I'm going to find out.*

His walk to the gym took him past the cruise

ships every day. And every day, he'd thought about just hopping onto one of them. Taking off—it didn't matter where. Every day, he wondered where his boat of choice would take him, what exotic places he'd find.

Now, with the girl, it seemed like fate.

It was spring break, his parents were in Europe, and there were still two long weeks left to his vacation. They'd never even know he was gone.

He couldn't just let the girl sail away, disappear on the blue horizon. Not now. Now that he'd seen her, he didn't want to let her out of his sight. She leaned over the railing, her eyes invisible behind dark sunglasses. Her smile was electric.

He watched as two crew members greeted the arriving passengers. One had a clipboard, while the other took tickets. Soon, the line had grown longer. He strolled closer. When no one was looking, he slipped past the security gate and raced up another gangplank—the crew's entrance.

If anyone asked, he was reporting for duty.

But no one asked.

He looked like any other college-age kid, working a job on spring vacation. Preppy. Good-looking. Sincere.

He looked back for a brief moment, but no one had noticed him heading aboard. Just before he entered the ship, he took one last glance upward at the girl. He couldn't resist.

The girl noticed him and smiled.

You like me, he thought, smiling back. *Good. Because I'm going to love you—whoever you are, whatever it takes. And once you're mine, I'm never, ever letting go.*

CHAPTER 1

⚖

Linda Sellers drew in a deep breath and threw open the door to the stateroom that was going to be her home for the next two weeks.

One long look, and she was able to let out that breath.

Decorated in shades of pink and gray, the room held two twin beds and a tiny sitting area with a couch, a TV, and VCR. To her right, she discovered the bathroom—more pink and chrome—with its full-size tub and shower.

"Pretty deluxe," she said, smiling at her cousin Carol, who was pushing through the door with her bags.

"Linda!" As Carol dropped her bags, her mouth fell open at the same time. "Deluxe is an understatement! This is luxury, especially compared to those awful inside staterooms. Gosh, you could sound at least a bit excited!"

Linda laughed. Inside, she was thrilled. She just wasn't like Carol—always showing her emotions to the world. "I *am* excited," she said. "Two weeks of cruising the most beautiful water in the world. Two weeks of sun and surf and working out—"

"Don't forget romance," Carol said emphatically. "Did you see the ship? There's a disco, a casino, gorgeous decks to lounge on. Linda, this cruise is all about falling in love!"

"Yeah, right," Linda said, laughing.

Carol was already in college and dated about as much as was humanly possible. The cruise was her idea. A way for Linda to forget Greg, her last boyfriend. The one who dumped her. Carol thought the cruise would be a great antidote to Linda's broken heart. Linda wasn't so sure. She certainly wasn't in the mood to meet guys.

The two cousins were going to be cruising the Caribbean for fourteen glorious days. Carol's travel agent had recommended seven days in the eastern Caribbean, back to Fort Lauderdale, then off again for another seven days in the west.

When Carol emerged from the bathroom holding up a very sexy black cocktail dress, Linda knew her cousin was serious about romance.

"What do you think?" she asked.

With her curly dark hair and shining brown eyes, Carol was a knockout.

"Incredible!" Linda said. "I'd better be ready to fend them off."

"Don't you dare, Linda Sellers," Carol said. "Or I'll never forgive you."

The cousins spent the next hour unpacking and dressing for dinner. Carol went for the knock-out punch and put on the black cocktail dress. Linda threw on a simple but flattering blue silk dress, along with a pair of strappy sandals that accentuated her long legs. After twisting her long red hair in a knot, she held it in place at the back of her neck with a black onyx chopstick. It was her trademark style, one that all the girls at school copied. Linda was just about ready when she spotted her astro-diary on the bed beside her open suitcase.

"Wait a sec," she said to Carol. "I want to check our horoscopes."

Carol emerged from the bathroom and tapped her foot impatiently. "I would never have bought you that diary if I'd known you'd use it to run your life!"

Linda laughed. Since Linda was a Capricorn, she liked things that were mystical. Carol was a

Gemini, the sign of the twins. That meant she was both romantic—and skeptical. She liked to hear her horoscope—especially if it included stuff about guys—but she didn't believe in it nearly as much as Linda.

Not that Linda had gone overboard. She just thought it was interesting how often the astro-diary was right. The morning Carol had called her about the cruise, her horoscope had predicted a change that might involve travel. And when Greg broke up with her, her astro-diary had been right there too—telling her that bad news was in the making, but that it would all be better for her in the end.

Better. Sure. In the end, maybe, but not now.

Linda sighed and tried to forget Greg for what felt like the millionth time.

I'm here to have fun, she thought, *not to wallow in breakup misery.*

"Here we go," she said, thumbing through the diary. "'Gemini. Do you fall in love too much? Is every guy fair game? If so, you might have an excess of Venus energy in your chart. Try pampering yourself instead of always looking for the next guy.'"

"Or I could try both," Carol said, applying her lipstick.

Linda laughed. Classic Gemini response. The twins. That was Carol.

"What do they mean by too much Venus energy?" Carol asked.

"It means you like nice things and nice men and you love to be in love," Linda told her. "You enjoy danger. Things like driving too fast and walking alone down dark streets."

"And you, being a levelheaded Capricorn, are a lot more practical than that," Carol guessed.

"Sometimes," Linda agreed. "Capricorns can be pretty romantic and dreamy, too. They just have to meet the right guy. And believe me, I mean *right*. To win us over, a guy has to be daring and confident. Money helps, too! We like guys to buy us nice things."

And treat us special, Linda thought.

Stop thinking about Greg, she told herself. *Carol has the right attitude. Look at her—the perfect dress, the perfect makeup, all excited about finding a date. I should be, too.*

"So what's in the stars for us tonight?" Carol asked.

Linda flipped through the pages of her diary. "Here we go. 'Look beyond the immediate,'" she read aloud. "'Feel free to travel and to love.'"

"Well, what do you know?" Carol turned from

the mirror. "That's exactly what I plan to do! So if you're ready, my dear practical cousin, let's head down to dinner and get started already!"

The *Libra* was a brand-new, state-of-the-art cruise ship, ten decks in all. There were staterooms on the three middle decks, with the sports deck above and entertainment and dining below. On the lower decks were more staterooms and the main dining room, where semi-formal dinners would be served each night. Linda couldn't wait to check out the pool, sauna, and gym on the sports deck.

"This boat has everything," Linda said to Carol. "Did you see the workout room? Two treadmills and a StairMaster. I'm going to be in the best shape of my life by the time we're home again."

"I can't believe you, Linda," Carol said. "Most people gain weight on cruises. You're talking about losing it. Who's going to keep me company while I'm pigging out at the Midnight Buffet?"

At the entrance to the dining room, Linda decided maybe Carol was right about the food. The smells were incredible. Almost as incredible as the room. Brass columns rose from plush carpeting of black, coral, and blue. Picture windows ran all along one wall, reflecting the sparkling lights of the chandelier and the candles set on each table.

"Wow," Linda exclaimed.

"Double wow," Carol agreed.

Two girls and a guy were already sitting at their table. The girl introduced herself as Justine Kellogg. Justine had thick, dark hair and warm brown eyes. When she smiled, which she did often, her face lit up.

"You'd never know it," Justine said to Linda and Carol, leaning over conspiratorially, "but I'm actually here trying to forget a guy."

"Me too!" Linda said. "Carol says a cruise is the worst thing to mend a broken heart—"

"Wrong," Justine said with a laugh. "What's better than to take a vacation from your problems?"

"Exactly. We'll lie in the sun, and swim, and work out—"

"And when we come back, our guys will be so devastated by how gorgeous we are, they'll want us back!"

Linda burst out laughing. So did the other girl, a tall blonde with flashing blue eyes and gorgeous cheekbones who was sitting to the right of Justine. "Go on, girl!" she said. "Now there's someone with the right attitude."

"Hey," said the boy on the other side of her. "Appreciate it."

The girl punched the boy lightly on the arm. Then she waved hello to Linda and Carol. "Don't mind him," she said. "He's British. He takes pride in his bad jokes. I'm Marla Robertson. This is my boyfriend, Kevin Malmstrom."

Kevin had gray eyes and the longest lashes Linda had ever seen. He wore his wavy brown hair long, to his ears, and parted down the middle. Linda thought immediately of a current British movie star. Kevin's looks had the same kind of boyish charm.

Linda had just finished introducing herself and Carol when a tall, dark-haired man in a white uniform approached their table.

"Good evening, everyone," the captain said in a low, softly accented voice, as sexy as his wavy dark hair and dark eyes. "I'm Jim Stamatakos, your captain. Sorry to be late, but I had some important business up on the bridge." With that, Captain Stamatakos took the remaining empty seat at the table. "It seems we have a slight problem onboard."

"Problem?" Carol asked. "What kind of problem? We're not going to sink, are we?"

"Sink?" Marla and Justine echoed. "The boat's sinking?"

The captain put a reassuring hand on Carol's

arm. Linda breathed a sigh of relief. Carol had sounded as if she was about to freak, and Linda was worried. Sometimes her cousin had a tendency to overreact. The captain must have noticed the high-pitched tone of her cousin's voice.

"Nothing like that," the captain said. He lowered his voice. "Actually, there's a stowaway onboard."

"A stowaway!" Carol echoed. "You're kidding!"

A stowaway. Linda scanned the dining room and felt her heart start to race. It could be someone in this very room. A chill passed over her as the captain went on.

"Unfortunately, a porter saw him sneaking aboard, but he was too far away to stop him. The fellow's disappeared—for now. But I'm sure we'll manage to catch him with your help."

"Our help?" Justine asked.

"I'm offering a reward," the captain said. "Whoever catches the stowaway will win a full day of beauty in the ship's spa. Or a round of golf at our first port. It's the least we can do."

Linda could tell the captain was trying not to make too big a deal of the stowaway. Even so, his face seemed tense beneath his smile. She scanned the crowd, only half-aware of the conversation at the table.

Someone in this very room had sneaked aboard.

Who?

And why?

It took a lot of guts to do something so risky. She didn't stop scoping the room when the waiter set a salad in front of her. Was it that man in the corner, the one with the dark hair and mustache? Or her? The young, thin woman flirting nervously with the guy at her table? She scanned the crowd a bit longer, collecting suspects in her mind. Capricorns loved a good mystery, and Linda was no exception. If nothing else, thinking about the stowaway would keep her mind off romance, especially now that Carol was so obviously into Captain Stamatakos.

And then she spotted *him.*

The one who made all her resolutions about guys and love and everything else disappear into thin air.

He had incredible green eyes, brown hair that curled down his neck, and a dynamite smile. From all the way across the room, she felt his eyes settle on her—and linger.

Linda caught her breath. She lowered her gaze and willed herself not to look.

Don't, she told herself. *He's not your type.*

Except that he was. With his long hair and his intense eyes, the guy was exactly her type. She felt her face grow hot, and wondered if he was still there. After a few moments, she dared to look up again.

He was gone.

Linda felt disappointment crash down around her. *I should just forget it,* she thought. *Unlucky in love, that's my problem. Stick to cards next time.*

She turned her attention back to the group. Kevin was talking about how he'd gotten from England to New York, where he'd met Marla.

"And I said to myself, now *there's* a smashing girl," he said, putting his arm around Marla.

"Smashing is right," said Marla, smiling up at him. "I was so busy staring at Kevin, I rear-ended the car in front of me!"

"That's a terrific story," Justine said, laughing loudly.

Not to mention romantic, Linda thought. When she looked up, her breath caught in her throat again.

He'd come back.

He stood about ten feet away from their table, leaning against a pillar, smiling. At her.

"Of course I offered to drive her to the hospital," Kevin said.

"Of course," said Justine.

"Even though there was nothing wrong with me," Marla put in.

"Of course," said Kevin.

"Linda?" Justine was saying. "Earth to Linda!"

Justine followed Linda's gaze.

And then the weirdest thing happened.

Justine stopped smiling. Her face turned deathly pale, and she looked as if she was about to pass out.

CHAPTER 2

"What's wrong?" Linda asked, tearing her eyes away from the hunk.

"N-n-nothing," Justine stammered. "I just don't feel so well." The girl's hands were shaking as she reached for her purse. "It must have been the scallops. My mother always told me never to eat scallops. Why don't I ever listen to her? Isn't that the way? They tell us not to do something and we do it anyway, and look what happens."

Justine shot up from the table and pushed her way through the dining hall. "Sorry!"

"Justine—" Linda stood up, ready to go after her. What had made her freak like that? Was it just the scallops? Then she felt the hand on her arm, holding her back.

"Don't leave," the voice said.

Linda turned.

And found herself staring straight into those incredible green eyes.

His eyes.

Without saying another word, he swept her onto the dance floor, his open hand firmly on her back. His touch made Linda weak in the knees. Gone was the practical Capricorn. Linda's dreamy side had kicked in—big time.

"I don't even know your name," she whispered.

"Billy Jackson," he said. "And you're Linda Sellers."

The hunk seemed to read her mind. "How do I know? Because the minute I saw you, I had to find out everything about you."

Linda's heart beat so fast, she could barely breathe. She didn't ask why, she didn't want to know. She just wanted to lose herself in Billy's arms.

The band changed songs, and Billy steered Linda into a faster beat. They danced for several more numbers, and when the band stopped for a break, Billy led Linda toward the open doors at the far end of the dining room.

A soft ocean breeze blew across the curtains and a full moon shone in the clear night sky. Without thinking, Linda and Billy found themselves wandering to the rail, to take in the warm spring night.

Linda drew in deep breaths and tried to slow down her fast heartbeat. The dancing had been incredible. But standing here at the rail…Everything she'd said about romance was about to go flying overboard. And Linda didn't care. Not one bit.

"It's gorgeous out here," she said.

"It sure is," Billy agreed. Without looking, Linda somehow knew he was staring at her instead of the stars. "So how did you find yourself on a cruise like this?" Billy asked, clearing his throat.

"My horoscope said I should travel," Linda said, laughing. "So I decided to travel."

"Your horoscope?"

Linda blushed and wished she could take back what she'd said. She hadn't even thought about it, and there she was, confessing to Billy she was into something flaky like astrology.

"I guess that came out wrong. What I meant to say—"

"You like astrology, too?" he asked.

Too?

Billy Jackson followed the stars?

"Actually, I do," she said. "You don't think that's weird?"

"Not at all." Billy's eyes lit up. "I think it's great. I totally believe in destiny, fate, all that stuff."

"Me too," said Linda in disbelief.

Billy reached for her hand. The touch sent another warm wave through Linda's body. "For example, don't you think it's possible that fate brought us together?" he asked softly.

She looked up at him and nodded, speechless. A lock of hair fell onto his forehead, and Linda wanted to push it away. She did.

"Sorry," she said, snatching her hand back immediately. "I didn't mean—"

"What?" he whispered. "To touch me? I'm glad you did."

"You are?" she asked.

"Yeah," he said.

"Why?"

"Because it gives me the excuse."

"To do what?"

"This."

And then he drew her to him, to hold her and kiss her.

For a long time, his lips lingered on hers, teasing her, drawing her out. Linda was breathless by the time the kiss was over. And ready for it to happen again.

"Wow," they both said at once.

"I guess that must be my Libra nature," Billy whispered, his cheek pressed lightly to hers, his arms wrapped warmly around her. He drew back to meet her gaze. "Impulsive, romantic, ruled by Venus."

Ruled by love.

"Which is sure to distract a Capricorn," she said.

"Capricorn, huh?" Billy twirled a stray strand of Linda's hair. "Well-organized, practical. So it *was* fate."

Linda felt her heartbeat start up again as Billy drew her lips toward his for another kiss.

"What was?" she murmured.

"That you'd meet a Libra, and fall in love."

"In love" wasn't exactly the way she'd put it. "Intensely interested" would be closer to the truth, but Linda wasn't in the mood for arguing. Instead, she lost herself in the music and the night and Billy's lips on hers.

The moment could have lasted forever, but a voice called out, "Hey, look at the two lovebirds. Billy Jackson, you sure don't waste any time."

Linda moved out of Billy's arms and saw a short, muscular guy coming toward them. The boy was dressed in jeans, a white T-shirt that showed off his terrific build, and a sports jacket. With him was Justine, who hung back a bit, smiling awkwardly at Linda and obviously a bit embarrassed at having caught her in the act. Marla and Kevin trailed behind, strolling arm in arm.

"Tommy! This is Linda. Who's your friend?" Billy asked.

"This is Justine," Tommy said. "I found her in the hall outside the dining room. I rescued her from the most boring man on this whole ship. So now she owes me her life, which she has agreed to give me. Justine, this is Billy."

"Hi, Justine."

Justine looked at Billy long and hard. Then she reached out to shake hands. "Hi, Billy," she said coolly.

The tone in her voice made Linda shiver. It was as if Justine was mad at her! But why? Because she had ditched Justine to be with Billy? For a second, Linda saw it the way Justine did: not half an hour ago, she'd been commiserating with Justine about what jerks guys could be. Now, here she was, nestled in the arms of Billy Jackson. Even so…they were on a cruise. Linda couldn't help it if she'd met a guy. She introduced Billy to Marla and Kevin to fill the silence.

"So," Tommy said, shoving his hands in the pockets of his jeans. "Did Billy tell you guys his big secret yet?"

"What secret?" Linda asked.

"It's nothing," Billy answered. "Really."

"Oh, I wouldn't call it nothing," Tommy offered. "Not exactly."

"What is it?" Linda asked.

Billy shot a look at Tommy, and Linda's heart beat a bit faster. Only this time, it wasn't excitement so much as nerves. Did Billy have another girlfriend? Was that what Tommy was trying to say?

"Why don't you tell me?" she asked.

"Sure," said Kevin. "Don't keep us all in suspense!"

"Linda and I just met. Maybe she doesn't want to know every last detail about me. At least not yet." Billy smiled awkwardly. "There's lots of time, right?"

Tommy held up his hands. "Sorry, man. I thought you'd be bragging about it the way you did with me." Tommy turned to Justine. "I'd met the guy five minutes—he came into the ship's gym, that's where I work—and already he's boasting about how he—"

This time, Billy's look was even more serious. Linda didn't miss it. Billy's expression was clear: Tommy should stop right now—while he was still ahead.

The tension between them was so strong, Linda decided the best thing to do was to back off. Which she was ready to do. But Marla wasn't the type of person to let something go easily.

"Come on, Billy," she said, teasing him with a poke in the stomach. "You can tell us."

Billy's lips clamped shut. Tommy just didn't seem to get the point. Instead, he smiled and pointed with his thumb at Billy.

"Since *he* won't tell you, I guess I'll have to. Billy's the stowaway."

CHAPTER 3

"You're kidding!" said Kevin, obviously impressed.

"No!" Marla gasped. "I love it! What a marvelous, brilliant idea! I wish I'd thought of it."

Linda's smile froze on her face. She wanted to agree with Marla, but she didn't see how stowing away was "brilliant."

She must have looked shocked, because right away Billy rushed to explain himself.

"Linda, I'm sorry. I was going to tell you. The truth is, my parents went off to Europe and left me behind. Gosh, I wasn't going to stick around at home by myself! Would you? Actually, I couldn't believe how easy it was. No one even tried to stop me."

The words all tumbled together in Linda's mind. While she listened to Billy's explanation, all she could think about was what a great time they'd

24

had dancing. And the kiss. She'd been totally interested in Billy. This had to be the worst thing she could possibly find out about him.

Or was it?

"Tommy's letting me hide out in a closet at the gym," Billy was saying.

"Tommy works on the boat," Justine pointed out. "Won't he get in trouble?"

"Nah," Tommy said with a shrug. "It's all pretty harmless, wouldn't you agree?"

"I'd say so," said Kevin. "We'll have a blast hiding Billy from Captain Jim. It'll be fun!"

"I'll say." Marla chuckled. "This cruise just got about ten times more interesting."

Linda listened to them talk and wondered if Marla was right. And then Billy turned to her and begged her with those intense green eyes of his.

"Linda?" he asked. "Can you deal?"

Can I deal?

Do I want to?

In the dark, with the warm breeze blowing off the ocean, the five of them looked at her expectantly. *Well?* they all seemed to ask.

She really liked Billy.

His eyes were imploring. *Don't ruin a good thing,* they seemed to say. *What's wrong with a little fun?*

What *was* wrong with a little fun?

A smile spread across Linda's lips. Capricorns could be about as daring as they were practical. She had to admit that a part of her—a pretty big part of her—found the idea of hiding Billy Jackson sort of exciting. Fun. An adventure.

"Sure," she said finally, drawing out the word.

Billy drew Linda to him and kissed her—hard. "So it's settled," he said. Taking Linda's hands in his, he asked, "Since you're the astrological expert, what are Tommy and Justine's chances for happiness?"

Justine's eyes lit up. Tommy turned out to be another Capricorn, which explained why he was so outgoing and athletic. Justine was born in early December, which made her a Sagittarius. That made sense, too, Linda explained, since from the minute they met Justine was friendly and up for almost anything.

"From what I remember, Capricorn and Sagittarius are a good combination," Linda told them. "Tommy, you probably like to blurt things out, right?"

Tommy made a face. "Maybe. So what?"

"So Justine won't mind," Linda explained. "Sagittarians can forgive almost anything."

"Almost," Justine said. "I can think of a few

things I haven't been able to forget. What about you and Billy?"

"I'm a Capricorn and Billy's a Libra."

"Which is why I fell for Linda the second I saw her," Billy said. "And why Linda's holding back."

Linda laughed. Billy was right. If anyone could make a Capricorn on the rebound get excited, it was a Libra.

"I thought Libra and Capricorn were a bad mix," Justine said. "Kind of like fire and water?"

"How can you say that?" Billy asked. "We just met!"

"What about us?" Marla asked. "I'm an Aries."

Linda took one look at Kevin's expensive clothes. "And Kevin's a Leo, right?"

"How'd you know?" Kevin asked, surprised.

Linda counted off the reasons. "Nice clothes, well-groomed, in love with an Aries. It wasn't too hard to figure out," Linda said, smiling. "You guys are perfect for each other. Practically soul mates."

"Wow," said Marla, impressed. "You're good."

It was getting late, so Tommy offered to walk Justine back to her cabin. Marla and Kevin strolled off, too, leaving Billy and Linda to linger on deck.

And linger.

In Billy's arms, Linda didn't want the evening to end. Even after he kissed her good night at her stateroom door, Linda could still feel her heart fluttering and the warm glow Billy's touch gave her.

Carol was still out. This time, Linda didn't envy her cousin's good luck. Linda had her own to think about.

She was floating on air as she got ready for bed. She was turning down the sheets when she spotted her astro-diary, tossed on the bed where she'd left it before dinner.

Before she met Billy.

It felt like a million years ago.

Since Justine's warning was still on her mind, Linda thumbed through the diary, looking up their charts.

"Capricorn and Libra: both leaders, both want to be in charge," the analysis read. *"Even worse, you both want to win. Be wary, and settle for a tie. Otherwise, be warned: the victory won't be sweet."*

Incompatible? Not quite. Competitive was more like it.

And Capricorns liked competition.

Linda put the book away, turned off the light, and smiled to herself. It sounded like fireworks were definitely possible. She wouldn't want it any other way. As she fell asleep, Linda thought about

Billy Jackson's lips on hers, and all her worries faded away.

"So, Tommy," Billy said at breakfast the next morning. "We really need to start thinking about this mutiny idea."

"Mutiny?" Linda said, holding her spoonful of strawberries midair. "What kind of mutiny?"

Billy and Linda were sharing a table with Justine and Tommy. Marla and Kevin hadn't appeared yet. Linda exchanged a look with Justine, who simply shrugged and went back to eating her yogurt.

"You're joking, right?" Linda said. She took a bite of the strawberries and swallowed. "Mutiny on a *cruise ship?* Why?"

"This isn't a joke, Linda." Billy leaned back in his chair. "There's every reason to mutiny on a cruise ship. Think about it! Why stop in all these boring places they have planned? Why not take over the ship and hit all the cool places? Secret coves, out-of-the-way islands. I mean, come on. Who really wants to go to San Juan, when there's an island like Martinique out there?"

Linda didn't want to admit it, but San Juan sounded pretty exotic to her. She'd never been to

Puerto Rico. When she thought about it, though, Billy had a point. It might be fun to take over the ship. Kind of like flying a jet plane and landing it wherever you wanted. She smiled at him, taking up his challenge.

"So what would you do?" she asked. "Where would you go?"

"Straight to Jamaica!" said Tommy. "We could pick up some serious, first-class rum."

"No, no, no," said Billy. "Boring, boring, boring. You're thinking small—you've got to think big. I say we steer the ship through the Bermuda Triangle. We'll be famous—if we survive."

"That's stupid," Tommy said, sulking. He was obviously mad at Billy for calling his idea boring.

"Stupid?" Billy said. "What's stupid is sailing to Jamaica for rum when we've got rum right here on this ship."

"It was just an idea," said Tommy.

"Tommy—" Justine put her hand on Tommy's arm. "Chill, okay?"

By now, Tommy's face was red and he was standing up, ready for a fight. Billy wasn't going to let Tommy bully him, though. He was taller than Tommy, even if he wasn't as muscular.

"I'll chill out when he apologizes," said Tommy.

"Relax," Linda told them both. "You guys are friends."

"I thought we were," said Billy. "But now I'm not so sure."

"Me neither," Tommy spat back.

With that, Billy lunged for Tommy.

"You guys!" Linda and Justine shouted.

Tommy was quick, but Billy was quicker. Tommy threw a punch. Billy ducked to avoid it, his green eyes filled with rage.

"No one tries to hit me!" he yelled.

Billy tackled Tommy to the ground. The boys rolled over and over, wrestling fiercely.

Then Billy got Tommy in a headlock. With his right arm, he pulled Tommy's head back, cutting off his breathing. Tommy's eyes bulged, but Billy just yanked harder.

Linda gasped in horror. Unless someone stopped him—fast—Billy was about to do some serious damage.

CHAPTER 4

And then the weirdest thing happened.

As quickly as he tackled Tommy, Billy let go.

Instantly, before Tommy's face could even return to its normal, tanned state, Billy was apologizing.

"I don't know why I lost my temper like that," he said, running a hand through his hair. "I'm sorry, man."

"It's okay," said Tommy. He got up, rubbing at his throat. Then he tucked his shirt back in and ventured a smile. "I think we both blew a fuse. Friends?"

They shook hands, and a few minutes later, it was as if nothing had happened. Billy let the mutiny line drop, and Tommy proved he didn't hold anything against Billy by offering to let him shower at the gym.

"Thanks, Tommy," said Billy. "You're a true bud."

The two went off together. Linda watched them leave, amazed that they'd both forgotten the nasty wrestling match so quickly. As if it had never happened. After they were gone, she exchanged a look with Justine, who simply shrugged and said, "Guys. Will we ever understand them?"

"Be careful of a Libra's tendency to control," Linda read in her astro-diary later that morning. *"He'll want to give you a ring and call you his own. Remember: Capricorn is ruled by Saturn. And we all know that planet has more than enough rings to go around. Capricorns should avoid at all costs wearing any jewelry on their fingers—it will only constrict!"*

Sounded like strange advice to Linda, but even so…She remembered what she'd read the night before, about how Libras and Capricorns would fight to the finish.

Definitely.

Billy had a temper, that was for sure. But so did she. Her face got red just remembering the last time she'd seen Greg. Boy, had she been angry. And boy, was that soda going to be hard to get out of Greg's nice white pants.

Not to mention Nadine's. Greg's new girl-friend. Seeing them in the mall—together—not two days after Greg had broken up with her had been enough to make Linda beyond mad. She was reeling. And she let him know.

At the memory of Greg's shocked expression, Linda smiled. At the thought of Billy's arms around her, Linda shivered in anticipation. Now that she had Billy, Greg was just a dim memory, getting even dimmer with each passing day.

"I can't believe how much time I'm spending with Billy," Linda wrote in her diary. *"Is it just a vacation thing, or will we see each other once the cruise is over? I wonder what Billy Jackson's like at home..."*

Linda was scribbling away when a shadow fell across the page.

It was Billy.

Quickly, Linda covered up the page.

"You write a lot of important stuff in there," Billy said, playfully trying to snatch the diary away. "Anything about me?"

Linda held on tightly to the book. "Maybe," she said, raising an eyebrow. "What if I do?"

"Then I'd say I'm flattered."

Billy kissed Linda about ten times, until she pushed him aside with a laugh. "Come on," she said. "Let's do something before dinner."

"Sure," said Billy. "How about a tour of the ship? I'll show you all the romantic spots."

Billy pulled Linda up from her seat. She collected her belongings and threw a silk robe on over her bikini. She was aware of Billy's appreciative eyes, and she had to admit—yet again—that it felt really good to have a guy so interested in her again.

"Hmm—" Billy nuzzled her neck. "Maybe we should just head back to your cabin. What do you say?"

"I'd say we spend more than enough time in my cabin," Linda replied, shoving him away lightly. "Besides, I still haven't seen where you're staying. I feel like you're keeping it a secret from me."

"Maybe I have a lot of secrets," Billy replied mysteriously. "Maybe you'll just have to stay with me forever, to find them all out."

Linda's heart beat faster. More than once, it seemed as if Billy was able to read her mind. Hadn't she just been wondering if she and Billy were going to keep seeing each other after the trip? Here he was, giving her a sign that he meant for them to be together once the cruise was over.

She'd heard about couples being able to read

each other's thoughts, but she'd never felt so connected to someone herself.

"I don't know about you, Linda," Billy was saying, "but I can't believe how fast this is going. I feel like we're meant to be together forever."

He'd done it again!

"I know what you mean," Linda said. "We only met two days ago, but already I feel closer to you than anybody else I've ever dated."

She reached up to put her arms around Billy's neck, and gazed longingly into his sea-green eyes. Then she let her lips move toward his in a kiss. When the kiss was over, Linda let out a long breath.

Wow.

Billy led her around the pool area to the bow of the ship, where the gym and spa were. The gym was pretty dead—there were only a few people working out. Billy took Linda's hand and quietly opened a door at the corner of the gym marked STAFF ONLY.

"Won't Tommy get angry?" Linda asked. But Billy put a finger to his lips, silencing her.

They were in a hallway. Supplies such as towels and cleaners were stacked on shelves. A door at the end of the hall looked locked, but Billy took out a key and opened it.

When Billy flipped on the lights, Linda found herself looking at a tiny mattress—no bigger than a workout mat—with a neat pile of clothes stacked next to it. There were some candy wrappers in a trash bag at the foot of the mattress, and a tiny pillow tossed against the wall.

"Home, sweet home," said Billy.

Linda drew in a breath. She'd never really thought about what Billy's life was like when they weren't together. Most of the time, she could even sort of forget that he'd stowed away. But looking at the mattress, she was reminded of just how dangerous it was for Billy to be onboard.

And just how exciting.

She'd never known someone like him. Someone who could just hop onboard a cruise ship, find somewhere to stay, and not seem too worried about it. Sleep in a closet and think it was all a great big adventure.

"It's pretty cozy, but I've been thinking I should move my things," Billy said with a casual shrug. "Probably even Tommy shouldn't know where to find me." He turned off the light and pulled the door shut. "It might get him in trouble. So I've got another place picked out. Want to see?"

"Sure," said Linda.

She followed Billy from the gym, down a long

corridor. Billy stopped short at a door marked UTILITY AREA. Then, using a credit card from his wallet, he snapped open the lock on the door. With a smile, he held the door open for Linda.

The door led onto a dark stairway.

"Go ahead," Billy said.

Linda hesitated. "Where are we going?"

"You'll see," said Billy.

The stairwell was dark and cold. Linda felt goose bumps rise on her arms. She remembered the sight of Billy's tiny mattress shoved into the closet, his neat pile of clothes. Her Capricorn love of adventure sent a shiver of excitement down her spine. Did she have what it took to keep up with a guy like Billy?

The expression in Billy's eyes seemed to be taunting her. So did the smile on his lips.

Of course she did. She wasn't a competitive Capricorn for nothing.

Eight flights later, Linda found herself far below deck, down where they could hear the ship's heavy machinery humming away. Billy directed her to a dark corridor, with a low-hanging ceiling. Small, bare bulbs lit the way.

"It's a secret passage," Billy explained. "I found it when I first came onboard. Ever since Tommy and I started thinking about taking over the ship, I've been spending my free time exploring. We'll need to know it inside out if we want to pull it off."

The corridor was sealed off every so often by huge metal hatches. Billy twirled the handle on the first hatch, opening it for her, then closing it behind him as they went through. After a long walk, they came to the very back of the ship. Two huge double doors led to a platform. There was an even larger hatch at the end of the platform, with a big, round window. Linda looked out and saw the darkening sea below.

"You know, I just realized something," Billy said with a smile. "We could hide Captain Jim down here. No one would find him in a million years. In fact, there's room for the whole crew. They'll be stuck down here, while we're upstairs, steering the boat, partying, having a great time."

Linda laughed. "That's a great idea," she said. "But what about Carol? She'll be miserable without the captain by her side."

"We'll let her visit," Billy said. "I'd hate to interfere with true love."

The platform was dark. Linda could hear the sea rushing against the keel below. Her heart started fluttering again, the way it always seemed to do around Billy. He stepped closer, so close she could feel Billy's breath on her face, his stomach pressed against hers. Then his lips were at her ear, planting tiny kisses there.

"We make a great team, Linda," he murmured. "Wouldn't you agree?"

Agree?

That was an understatement.

And then he was reaching for her, drawing his lips toward hers, covering his mouth with hers.

When the kiss was over, Billy's eyes were dancing. "And to prove how I feel about you, I want to show you something. Something really important."

"I think you've shown me enough today," said Linda with a laugh. "But okay. Why not?"

Above deck, Billy squired Linda toward the main lobby. "I want you to pick something out," he said, pointing to the ship's boutique. "A present. Anything you want."

Linda stopped short. She and Carol had gone into the boutique only once—and walked out again five minutes later, laughing about how they couldn't even afford to browse. Anything Billy bought her there would cost a lot.

"I'm not sure," she said.

"Come on." Billy held the door open for Linda to go inside. "Just pick something out. It would really mean a lot to me."

There were glass cases full of gorgeous rings and watches, racks of expensive clothes and accessories. Diamonds winked under the soft light. Rich gold bands sparkled. The saleswoman stood back, waiting for them to decide what they wanted to see. But Linda felt awkward. There weren't even any price tags!

"I can't—"

Billy pointed to an expensive pearl comb. "That would look great in your hair," he said.

Linda fingered the chopstick she wore every day. Then she had an idea. Billy liked a challenge. She'd give him one. "Why don't *you* pick something out?" she said. "Surprise me."

His eyes lit up. "That's a great idea. Get going. I'll meet up with you at dinner."

Linda waved good-bye and floated off. She was utterly overwhelmed by everything about Billy. His sense of adventure, how romantic he was. What a great kisser…

Back in her cabin, Linda didn't notice the note until she closed the door behind her. At first, she thought it was a piece of trash on the floor. But then she bent over to pick it up—and saw her name.

Linda unfolded the note. From the first words, she felt her heart stop short.

Your Billy has a secret. Libra's a double sign, isn't it? That means there are two sides to every story. Beware.

CHAPTER 5

Linda awakened the next morning to the sounds of shouts and yells.

She shot out of bed.

The sun was blazing through the porthole. The bed beside her was empty.

Carol was gone.

Something was wrong.

With a jolt, Linda realized what had changed.

The ship wasn't moving. They'd docked!

She peered out the porthole to discover a glorious view of San Juan harbor. Stalls selling clothes and crafts lined the pier. Looming above the harbor was the old walled fortress she'd seen in her guidebook.

Linda looked at the alarm clock and realized it was already eleven. She'd completely overslept!

She and Billy had stayed up late dancing with

Marla and Kevin, Justine and Tommy. She'd been having too good a time to worry about the note, but as she was getting dressed, she found it and read it again.

Billy had a "secret"?

What kind of secret?

For a moment, a cloud seemed to pass over the sunny day. But a second later, her practical Capricorn side kicked in. *There's no point in worrying about it,* she told herself. The note probably just came from someone who was jealous of her and Billy, and wanted to ruin her good time. It was silly anyway. *Two sides to every story?* Come on!

Linda shrugged and shoved the note into the desk drawer. It was too gorgeous a day to worry about some stupid note. Instead, she quickly finished dressing and left her cabin.

At the rail of the promenade deck, other passengers stood waiting for the gangplank to be lowered. Marla and Justine were there. "Justine and I are heading ashore to do some serious shopping. Want to come along?"

"Sure," said Linda. Just standing at the rail made her excited to check out the town.

The girls were getting ready to leave the boat when Billy came along. He drew Linda aside and handed her a small package. She recognized the purple-and-gold wrapping of the ship's boutique. Her heart started beating faster.

"Open it," Billy urged.

Linda's hands were shaking as she unwrapped the paper. Inside, she found a small, velvet box. The kind of box that held engagement rings. Her hands shook even more, and she held her breath, afraid to open it.

"You didn't," she said.

"No, I didn't," Billy confessed. "But I wanted to."

When she flipped open the box, Linda saw a thick silver band set with three stones. "It's gorgeous."

"See," said Billy. "There's a red stone to match your hair, a blue one since sapphire is one of Capricorn's colors, and a green one—"

"To match your eyes," Linda said, kissing him. "I love it."

And then a strange thing happened. Billy went to put the ring on Linda's finger, but instead of feeling happy, Linda felt a chill come over her. Suddenly, she couldn't concentrate on Billy, or the ring, or his hand in hers. Instead, she kept hearing a voice warning her—

He'll want to give you a ring and call you his own...

The other day she'd given Billy a spare key so that he could shower in her room. Did Billy use the key to sneak in and read her diary?

Put on the ring, Linda. Till death do us part.

He was just giving her a ring. It didn't necessarily *mean* anything at all.

Linda spun the ring on her finger. *It must be the note,* she thought. *Maybe it did bother me, more than I knew.*

Billy smiled at her. "Is something wrong?" he asked.

Linda smiled back. "No," she said. "Not at all."

Billy pecked her on the cheek. "Good. Because I have a surprise for you later. Meet me back here at four. And don't forget your bikini."

Linda had a great time with Marla and Justine. They shopped and ate a terrific lunch. By four, she was back in her cabin, dropping off the souvenirs she'd bought. There, she found a gorgeous bouquet of a dozen roses, and a note from Billy.

> The mutiny is on.
> Love, Billy.

Linda's pulse quickened. Mutiny? Was Billy serious? Was this the surprise he'd planned? She put on her sexiest bathing suit and was on deck at four. Maybe there was still time to talk him out of it.

He was there, just as he said he would be. Right on time. She wasn't surprised.

"What's going on?" she asked expectantly.

Billy held a finger to his lips. "Shh," he said. "We don't want to ruin it by having anyone find out."

"Are we really taking over the ship?" she asked. "Do you think—"

"Maybe." Billy's smile gave nothing away. He led her around to the stern of the boat. There, he climbed over a low wall, helping Linda follow him onto a narrow ledge between the ship and the lifeboats.

She gave him a questioning look. Billy smiled and crouched down. Then he pulled back a white canvas tarp to reveal an expensive speedboat. It was attached to the ship with ropes and pulleys, just like the lifeboats on either side of it. Only the speedboat was chained to the ship—locked up tight.

"Billy!" Linda said, her eyes wide in surprise. "What are we doing here?"

"This is Captain Jim's launch. We're just going to borrow it for a few hours."

"You're crazy!" Passengers strolled the deck all around them. "That's stealing!"

"Not if you return it."

By now, Billy had managed to unlock the padlock with a tiny key. Linda's excitement rose. She didn't even want to think about how he'd gotten his hands on the key. Instead, she watched in amazement as Billy used the ropes to lower the boat off the side of the ship.

"Tommy and I found some scuba equipment," Billy whispered to Linda as he worked. "We stashed it in the speedboat last night. I've got a hot tip on a great diving location, too. It's now or never, Linda. Are you coming or not?"

Linda took a last glance around. Billy had already decided he was going off in the speedboat. What was the point of her hanging around the ship once he was gone?

"No one will catch us," said Billy. "Come on!"

By now, the boat was floating in the water. "Climb the ladder and jump into the boat," he told her. "Are you chicken?"

Was he kidding?

"Of course not," said Linda. Her heart beat triple time as she climbed down the ladder, then let herself fall into the boat. A second later, Billy had landed beside her, a big smile on his face.

"Incredible," she said, shaking her head. "What will you come up with next?"

With one hand on the speedboat's steering wheel and the other around Linda's waist, Billy took them out of the busy harbor, full of cruise ships and sailboats, and south along the coast. Soon, they were passing by tiny, secret coves. The blue-green sea was calm. Farther out, a curl of white foam crested on a reef.

"Didn't I tell you this was a great idea?"

Billy pulled into a cove where the beach was empty. *It's our beach,* she thought. *We have it all to ourselves.* He cut the engine and dropped the anchor. Linda let her feet dangle over the side of the boat in the warm water. The water was so clear, Linda could see schools of brightly colored tropical fish swimming by. She couldn't wait to see them up close during her dive.

"All set," Billy told her, handing over the tank and mask.

There was only one tank. "You're not coming?" Linda asked.

Billy shrugged. "You go first. I'll dive afterward. Tell me how it is," he added with an encouraging smile.

Linda put on the gear, then sat at the edge of the boat. Billy gave her a big thumbs-up. "Go for it."

She let herself fall backward into the warm, tropical water. It felt so good to dive!

All sorts of incredible fish swam alongside her. Linda spotted a sea turtle swimming out from behind a stand of coral. She let herself drift for a while, just watching the sea life around her. Then she started swimming with the fish, diving lower toward the seabed. Along the way, she spotted shrimp and crabs scuttling by. In the distance, there was a large fish swimming toward her. A dolphin, maybe?

Were there sharks in the waters here?

Linda held her breath for a moment, wondering if she should keep on going or head up to the surface. She decided not to risk it, and began to climb upward.

She kept one eye on the large fish and the other on the glistening surface of the water, high above her head.

She was still almost fifty feet from the top when her breather shut down.

Linda panicked. She sucked on the mouthpiece.

Nothing.

It couldn't be true.

But it *was* true.

Her tank was out of air.

The surface was still thirty feet up.

There was no way she was going to make it.

She was going to drown.

As panic took over, all she could think was, *I'll never see Billy again.*

CHAPTER 6

Linda clawed her way to the surface. Her lungs were burning for air. Just a second earlier, the ocean had seemed like an underwater paradise. Now, it had turned deadly. Suffocating.

She burst through the water to gulp down lungfuls of air. Billy was leaning over the side of the boat, watching her intently.

"How did it go?" he asked.

"How could you?" Linda sputtered. "You let me go down there without enough air."

"What are you talking about?" Billy said. "I checked the tank myself."

Linda crawled aboard the boat, exhausted and defenseless. "Check it again," she told him. "Because I couldn't draw a single breath out of it. I thought I was going to drown."

Billy helped Linda take off her gear. One look at the tank's regulator told Billy that Linda was right. There was no pressure. The oxygen was gone.

"You're wrong, Linda," Billy insisted. "If you think I'd do something like this, then you just don't know me very well."

Linda took a long look at Billy. He nervously pushed a strand of hair away from his face and clenched his jaw. "It was an accident," he insisted. "The tank failed."

For a long moment, they stared at each other. Then Billy jammed on the ignition and pulled the boat out of the cove—at about a hundred miles an hour.

Linda felt awful. Of course Billy had been right. Of course it was an accident.

"Billy, listen, I'm sorry," she said. "It's just that I know how everything is one big adventure to you—"

"An adventure is one thing," Billy said angrily. "You're saying I'd do something that would hurt you. Maybe even kill you. I can't believe you'd think that about me. I love you, Linda. I'd never in a million years do something to hurt you."

He loved her?

"I know you wouldn't," she said. She tried to put her arms around him, but Billy pulled away stiffly.

"I don't believe you," he said.

Billy raced them back to the boat. Linda wasn't worried that someone might see them coming back in Captain Jim's launch. She was thinking about the accident and what Billy had said. She was still in a daze as Billy got them safely aboard and hoisted the boat back into its spot, without their being noticed. The whole time, he said no more than about two words to Linda.

For the first time, he didn't kiss her good-bye.

Linda walked back to her cabin alone, completely confused. She took a long, hot shower, hoping it would help her make some sense out of what had happened. When she got out of the shower, she picked up the phone and called the gym. Tommy answered on the second ring.

"Hey, it's Linda."

"Hi. What's up? How was your dive?"

"Pretty awful, actually. My tank ran out of air."

"You're kidding. Listen, hold on a second, okay?" There was a brief pause while Tommy answered someone's question about a weight. "Linda, I can't believe that. I told Billy—" Tommy stopped himself.

"You told Billy what?" Linda asked.

"Nothing," Tommy said. "Hey, I gotta go, okay? I'll see you later."

The dial tone in Linda's ear buzzed loudly. What had Tommy been about to say?

That he'd told Billy not to play that trick on her?

That he told Billy it would be a mistake?

That Linda might drown?

I'm totally overreacting, she thought as she replaced the receiver. *Billy's crazy about me. He'd never do anything to hurt me.*

But she caught herself staring at Billy's ring, and the astro-diary's advice echoed in her ears.

Be careful of a Libra's tendency to control.

When the phone rang, Linda jumped a mile. "Hello?" she said.

It was Billy.

"Did you notice, Linda?"

His voice was soft and smooth, registering none of the tension between them. It was as if he'd completely forgotten about their fight. As if he was two different people.

A Libra.

"There were only eleven roses in the bouquet I sent you," Billy went on. "If you want the twelfth, meet me on the deck in ten minutes."

He hung up before she could say no.

That was Billy. Always charming, always confident.

Always able to make her heart beat just a little faster.

See, she told herself. *Nothing's wrong at all.*

Linda ran a comb through her wet hair and fastened it with her chopstick. Then she grabbed her purse and headed for the deck. Billy was waiting with a smile on his lips and a single red rose in his hand.

"Do you know what a single rose symbolizes? Perfection," he said, placing it in her hand. Then he wrapped his fingers around hers and said, "I'm sorry."

"I'm sorry, too," said Linda. "I don't know what I was thinking—"

"I lost my temper, Linda," Billy went on. "It's just that I hate to have you think anything bad about me. I know I've done some stupid things, and I know I can't always control my anger. But you know I'd never hurt you, don't you?"

Linda looked deep into his intense green eyes.

"Don't you?" he repeated.

Of course she did.

That night, Billy had tickets to a concert onshore.

The band was a really popular reggae group from Jamaica. The crowd was hopping, the night was warm, the music was great.

There was only one problem. Billy couldn't get six seats together. Three seats were in one row, and three in a row behind.

"You, Justine, and Tommy can hang out up front," said Billy. "Marla, Kevin, and I will sit behind you."

"Okay," said Linda, trying to hide her disappointment. Billy had been pretty quiet all night. Linda was starting to feel as if he was giving her the cold shoulder and she couldn't figure out why.

It didn't help that she'd made the mistake of sitting between Tommy and Justine. For some reason, Tommy was in a really talkative mood. And for some reason, Justine wasn't. So Linda ended up having to keep up a conversation with Tommy while Justine shot daggers at both of them. It wasn't that Linda didn't like Tommy. She did. But like most Capricorns, Tommy liked to say silly, off-the-cuff things.

At one point, he leaned over and whispered in her ear, "You don't really love Billy, do you? How about running off with me?"

"Tommy—" Linda was aware of Justine sitting right next to her. Had she heard him? "Cut it out.

Let's listen to the band, okay?"

For a while after that, Tommy was quiet, but then he started joking with her again. "Really. I've got money too. I can buy you lots of nice things. How about it?"

"I don't think so," said Linda. What about Justine? Was he crazy? "Cool it, okay?"

For Linda, the concert was turning into a disaster. Tommy was stressing her out, Justine was getting madder by the minute, and Billy was no help whatsoever. It seemed as if every time Linda turned around, Billy was laughing and giggling with Marla. Obviously, he was trying to make her jealous. Well, it was working.

Maybe she should flirt with Tommy after all. Maybe that would make Billy sit up and take notice.

"Linda—" Marla leaned toward their seats. "Has Billy ever told you about how he once dated this girl—"

"Marla!" Billy's voice was sharp, angry. "I told you, cut it out."

Marla turned to give Billy a look. "You can't tell me what to do," she said. "I'm not one of your *girlfriends*." Marla leaned on the word as if she knew exactly what it was like to go out with Billy.

Wait a minute, Linda thought. Marla said *girlfriends*, not *girlfriend*. What was that all about?

But she didn't have time to wonder.

Billy was too busy changing the subject. He wanted to talk about his mutiny plan to take over the ship. He leaned forward and told Tommy about how he'd been studying the staff schedule. "At night, the only guy on the bridge is someone named Terry Pendlebury. He's the staff captain. Everyone else, including Captain Jim, is off duty. Piece of cake, wouldn't you say?"

Tommy frowned. "I don't know. The only way we can really take the bridge is to cause some kind of diversion." Tommy thought for a moment. "Maybe we could sabotage the engine room or something like that."

"Maybe," Billy agreed. "The problem is, we don't know anything about engines."

"True," said Tommy. "How about opening one of the hatches? Letting the ship take on some water?"

Linda was surprised as she listened to the conversation. "You guys are really serious about this mutiny thing," she said.

"Of course we are." Billy smiled in her direction. "Tommy's right. What we need is a distraction. And I think I have just the one."

The others wanted to know what Billy had planned, but he wasn't about to tell them. "It's a secret," he said. "I want you all to be surprised."

The six friends got back to the boat late. By the time she was in bed, Linda was completely exhausted. She didn't even have the energy to open her astro-diary, even though she had a lot she could write about. Her mind was racing with everything that had happened. And yet she was totally exhausted. She drifted off...

And three hours later, she shot up with a jolt.

Her cousin's screams were in her ear.

"Linda, wake up! The ship's sinking! We're going down!"

CHAPTER 7

Six long steamer blasts cut through the silent night.

Six short ones followed.

The sounds were loud and hollow. Terrifying.

"All hands on deck!" came the captain's voice on the public address system. "Emergency! All hands on deck!"

Carol was hysterical. "We're going to drown," she sobbed. "Oh, Linda, we're going to die."

"Shh!" Linda gathered her cousin in her arms and threw open the door. Alarms were going off in the halls. Red lights flashed along the ceiling. Dazed passengers stood at their doors, confused expressions on their faces.

"What is it?" a woman asked. "What's going on?"

"We're sinking," Carol said again. "The ship's going down!"

At Carol's announcement, a man let out a long groan and the woman standing next to him began to cry hysterically. Other passengers rushed back to their rooms to put on life vests, and started heading out to the deck.

"Carol, cut it out," Linda said sharply. "We're not going to drown. What makes you say the ship is sinking?"

"Do you hear those steamer blasts?" Carol said. "That's the warning, Captain Jim told me. Six long ones, followed by six short ones. It means the boat's sinking!"

The steamer blasts continued. While the other passengers raced for the lifeboats, Linda hurried back inside their stateroom and emerged with two life vests. She made Carol put one on over her nightgown, and did the same herself. Then she dragged her cousin down the hall and out to the deck.

"All passengers please proceed to the mustering stations," came the captain's voice. "Please move quickly and with caution."

Linda didn't know what mustering stations were, but she quickly found out. All around the deck, crew members gathered groups of passengers together, checked their life vests, and made sure everyone remained calm. The captain went from group to group. He looked concerned—and scared.

Linda and Carol moved toward one of the groups. Just as they were about to join the crowd of agitated passengers, Linda caught sight of Billy, standing off to the side.

Billy didn't seem worried.

Billy wasn't even wearing a life vest. Instead, he was grinning from ear to ear.

For some reason, Billy was happy.

"Isn't it exciting?" he said, coming over to Linda and Carol. "Can you believe it? It's just like the *Titanic!*"

Carol shot Billy a deadly look. "I don't know what you're so happy about. We're going to drown! Doesn't that mean anything to you? I suppose you can swim. Well, I can't—"

"Actually, I'm a terrible swimmer," Billy said.

His grin widened.

Linda watched him in amazement, and she knew, even before the captain made his announcement, that the ship wasn't sinking after all. That they'd all been jolted awake by a false alarm. That the six long blasts and the six short ones had been set off by someone who knew it was the emergency signal, someone who didn't care about waking up the whole ship in the middle of the night. Or making them all fear for their lives.

Which also explained Captain Jim's concern, and his fear. He knew that *someone* had set off the alarm. He just didn't know who.

But Linda did.

She knew exactly who it was.

Billy Jackson.

The next day, Linda avoided Billy. After the episode with the lifeboat drill, she was more than tired of his pranks. She was actually angry. Stealing the captain's launch was fun, but people had gotten really upset during the drill. Billy's tricks weren't innocent. They were dangerous.

Billy found her that afternoon, taking some sun on the promenade deck. He flopped down on a lounge chair next to her. After pecking her lightly on the lips, he pushed the fisherman's cap he was wearing up on his head.

"So are you ready?" he asked.

"For what?" she wanted to know.

"For the mutiny. Last night was just a dry run. Tommy and I are putting the finishing touches on our plan. It's all set to go."

Linda sighed. "Billy, listen—"

"Everything's worked out," he said. "We're going to run another drill. This time, Tommy'll be right outside the captain's door. As soon as the captain comes out, he'll knock him flat and take him to that spot belowdecks. It's going to be a cinch."

"Billy, last night wasn't a joke," Linda said. "People were afraid. Maybe taking over the ship isn't such a great idea. We don't even know how to run it! And where are we going to go? We can't keep the captain down in the hold forever. What about the rest of the crew? This isn't a joke, you know."

Billy stared at her in disbelief. "Linda, you're not backing out, are you? Either you're in this with me, or—"

"Or what?" Linda asked.

"Or you're not," Billy said simply.

Linda's eyes narrowed. The challenge wasn't just about the mutiny—it was about them.

This is who I am, Billy seemed to be saying. *If you can't play along, then maybe you should get out of the game.*

And maybe he was right.

"Maybe we should take a break from each other," Linda suggested slowly. It was only when the words came out that she knew for sure how she felt. "We've been spending a lot of time together."

"A break?" Billy asked, his voice rising. "What do you mean by that?"

"I don't know," Linda said in exasperation. Why did Billy have to make everything so difficult? "It's just that we've gotten really tight really fast, and I'm feeling like I need some time to myself."

Tommy and Justine strolled by, along with Marla and Kevin. Tommy and Kevin gave them both a big hello, while Justine and Marla kept on walking. The girls sat down on some deck chairs, just out of earshot. Kevin and Tommy joined them.

"Space?" Billy repeated. "For what? So you can date other people? Like my best friend, for example? I saw you flirting with him at the concert. Why do you think I was being so friendly with Marla? Because I could tell there was something going on between you and Tommy. Admit it, Linda. Wasn't there?"

Not unless you count Tommy coming on to me, Linda wanted to say. She looked over at Tommy and Justine. They were obviously enjoying her fight with Billy. When Tommy saw Linda glance his way, he pretended not to be listening.

✸

"Billy, you're wrong about the other night. I wasn't flirting with Tommy. Listen, all I'm saying is that I want to slow things down. There's nothing wrong with that, is there? We're on a terrific vacation, and there's lots to do. I've hardly even spent any time with my cousin."

"That's not what this is about," said Billy. "Not at all. It's about you and me, and how you're not ready to go along with the plan. I thought you were up to it, Linda, but it's obvious you're not. And since you're not, maybe we should just forget about us."

Linda was stunned.

Billy was breaking up with *her*?

"Okay," she said slowly. "If that's how you feel." She took off her ring and handed it back to Billy. "I'm sorry it had to end up this way."

Billy's hand was warm when Linda pressed the ring into it, but his eyes were cold. Linda walked away. She'd only gone a few feet when something flew by her and bounced off the ship's metal side.

The ring.

She turned to look at Billy, who stood with his fists by his side. "I'll make you pay for this, Linda Sellers. We had a perfectly good thing going. And no one messes up a perfect thing without being sorry in the end."

CHAPTER 8

♎

There's nothing scarier than a lonely Libra.

    Billy won't leave me alone. He says he made a big mistake, didn't know what he was saying, is devastated. Sure he is. But now that I'm not spending my every waking minute with the guy, I'm starting to think I may be better off

"Hey, Linda!" Kevin called out to Linda from across the deck. "We're heading ashore. Want to join us?"

    Marla was with him, wearing a floppy straw hat and a flowered sundress.

    "There's a great beach we want to find," Marla said. "We're going to rent mopeds. Come on—it'll be fun."

    "No thanks!" Linda waved them off. "Go ahead. And have a great time."

Linda still didn't feel entirely comfortable spending a lot of time with Kevin and Marla. Three was definitely a crowd where they were concerned. But Marla had tried to be really nice to Linda ever since Billy had broken up with her. Even Justine seemed to have forgotten her grudge. At breakfast that morning, she'd asked Linda if she wanted to take an aerobics class with her. Linda hadn't felt up to it, but she was glad Justine had asked.

Linda sighed and went back to writing in her diary.

on my own.

Being with Billy made me feel really special. But I don't know—maybe that was my mistake in the first place?

"You write a lot of important stuff in there," a voice said. Linda looked up to see Billy smiling at her, holding out a red rose. "Anything about me?"

"Haven't I heard that before somewhere?" Linda asked him.

"You never answered me."

"The answer is no. I don't write anything about you in here." Linda slammed the diary shut, hiding her slightly red face. "What is it,

Billy? What do you want?"

"You know what I want, Linda," he said, sitting at the edge of her deck chair. "I want you."

Linda pushed back a strand of hair that had blown across her face. "Well, that's not going to happen."

"Why not?" Billy asked. "I don't want to beg, Linda, but won't you even think about us getting back together again?"

"How long have we known one another, Billy? Five days. Tops. You'll forget about me. The minute this cruise ends and you're not seeing me every day, I'll just be some girl you met." Linda gathered her diary, her towel, and her sunscreen and got up to leave. "Get over it, Billy. Because I have."

It killed her to be so mean to him, but Linda knew it was the only way.

In an all-out war, settle for a draw.

Hadn't her astro-diary warned her in the first place? Did she really want a fight to the finish?

Linda turned back to see Billy staring after her.

Apologize, Linda, something inside her said.

Before it's too late.

All that day, Linda saw Billy practically every time she turned a corner. She'd be getting out of the pool, feel Billy's eyes on her, and look up to see him staring at her from the deck. Or at breakfast. There was Billy, across the room, following her with his eyes.

"Following her" was probably an exaggeration, Linda decided. But it seemed as if wherever she turned, there was Billy Jackson.

Staring at her.

Smiling at her.

Trying to talk to her.

Telling her it had all been a misunderstanding.

All the time, Linda wondered if she was making a mistake. Maybe she should get back together with him. Except a funny thing was happening. Billy seemed to be falling apart. He wasn't looking too good, for one thing. Gone were the clean white oxfords and the pressed chinos. Gone was the sweet-smelling, sexy, handsome man Linda had fallen for. Instead, Billy wandered the ship dressed in cutoffs and a dirty T-shirt. Tommy's clothes, Linda recognized. His hair was unwashed.

Libra transformed, without his Venus.

Linda realized that since she wasn't letting him into her cabin to shower, Billy probably had nowhere to wash up. She'd been putting his clothes in with hers to go to the laundry. But no more. Now Billy couldn't dress with his usual flair. She asked Tommy about it at dinner that night, and he admitted that he'd had to kick Billy out of his hiding place at the gym. The captain was getting serious about finding the stowaway before the cruise ended, and Tommy didn't want to risk getting into trouble.

"Besides, Linda," Tommy confided in her. "I'm a little worried about him. Billy's really into this mutiny thing." Tommy leaned in closer. "He's waiting to pull it off because he wants you back on his side. But he's serious. He says he knows where Captain Jim keeps his gun."

That was serious. Linda bit on a fingernail.

Even Tommy looked concerned. "Should we turn him in?"

It seemed drastic. "Billy would kill us," she said. "I mean, can't we just wait and see what happens?"

"I guess," said Tommy. "Maybe nothing will happen."

Somehow, he didn't sound convinced.

Somehow, Linda wasn't convinced either.

The footsteps were getting closer. And closer. Linda was running as fast as she could, but there was no escaping them.

She turned a corner and slipped on the ship's darkened, slippery deck.

Linda clutched the rail for balance. She pulled herself up.

The footsteps had stopped.

She willed herself not to turn around.

He was still there. Waiting. In the dark.

Slowly, Linda began walking toward her room. The footsteps started again. She began to run. The footsteps went faster.

She turned around.

He was there.

Billy.

Even in the dark, she could see his flashing green eyes, burning into her.

"You're mine, Linda," he said. "Don't you see?"

Linda tripped and went sliding across the deck. Strong hands reached out to grab her. It was Billy.

He wrapped his arms around her and drew her to him. His lips were chapped and rough, his breath stale. Suddenly, his hands tightened like metal clamps.

Linda struggled to get free.

"Stop," she cried. "You're hurting me."

"That's the point, Linda," Billy said. "Don't you realize? If I can't have you, no one will."

*   *   *

Linda awakened with a jolt.

It was only a dream.

A nightmare, she corrected herself.

Her heart was pounding and her mouth was dry. In her head, she could still hear Billy's awful voice. And when she closed her eyes, she could still see his twisted features.

She was so upset, she didn't realize that the door was open and the room was full of light from the hallway.

Someone had been here.

Shivering in fear, Linda got up to close the door. The hallway outside was empty. A breeze blew through the corridor.

Just the wind, she told herself. *It's only the wind.*

When she turned to go back to her room, Linda saw the pages of her diary flipping open in the breeze.

Across the last entry, someone had left a note.

Not *someone.*

Billy.

Imperfect, he'd written across the page.

CHAPTER 9

"Sounds like the curse of the *Libra* to me," Carol said at breakfast the next morning. She took a sip of her coffee. "Remember what Captain Jim said the other night at dinner?"

Did she ever. Jim had been talking about the false alarm. He'd told Carol and Linda how over the years some passengers had come to believe that the ship was cursed, and he was starting to wonder if maybe it was true.

"You think Jim is right?" Carol asked, suppressing a laugh.

Sure he is, Linda thought. *The curse of the Libra. And I know exactly which one.*

Carol must have seen the worry in her face. "Linda, be serious. Is there *any* reason to think Billy's dangerous?"

Linda hesitated. Now was the time to tell Carol

that Billy was the stowaway. But she still couldn't bring herself to turn him in. If Billy was upset enough about breaking up with her to sneak into her room at night while she was sleeping, she hated to think about what he might do to her if she told the captain about him.

"Not necessarily," Linda said finally. "It's just that I'm scared. It's creepy to think about a guy breaking into your room, don't you think?"

"That depends on what he has in mind." Carol winked. "It could be romantic, if it's the right guy. But seriously, Linda. You're worrying about nothing. Billy's the one who broke up with you. Why would he be trying to hurt you?"

Linda realized Carol was right. "I sound crazy, don't I?"

"Just a little. The sanest thing you've said so far is that we've only got a week left in the cruise. Now that's serious!" Carol got up from the table. "Seven more days to enjoy ourselves. Time's running out. Why don't we head ashore today and do some shopping? It's better than sitting around the pool all day writing in that diary of yours, isn't it?"

Carol was right. The ship had docked in Saint Martin, and Linda left the ship with her cousin to explore Philipsburg. Carol found a great price on her favorite French perfume. Linda picked up a beautiful leather purse. The sun beat down on her bare shoulders, and the air smelled of sweet flowers.

Billy Jackson should have been a distant memory.

Except…

All day, Linda had the definite impression that someone was following her.

It wasn't something she could really put her finger on. She was leaving a shop when she saw a shadow out of the corner of her eye.

Was it Billy?

Linda turned around, quickly searching up and down the street.

Nothing except a few cars and some pedestrians. A calm, cobblestoned street. Quaint. And safe. Or was it?

Maybe he was hiding in the doorway to one of the shops. Maybe he'd just turned the corner. All Linda knew was that she felt the same way she did when she'd look up in the dining room and see Billy's eyes upon her. Billy staring at her.

Only this time, no one was there.

Linda shook off the feeling. Carol dragged them down the street to an art gallery. In the window were paintings of big, bold figures, painted in bright oranges and reds. Carol loved the art and hurried inside to buy a poster for Captain Jim. Linda remained on the street, and her thoughts kept straying to Billy.

A tall, dark-haired boy strolled by, about Billy's height and Billy's age. Linda held her breath and stepped back into the doorway. He had the same longish hair trailing onto his neck.

Was it Billy?

The boy ambled past, giving Linda a big smile as he went by.

No.

Not Billy at all.

Get a grip, Sellers, she told herself. *You're losing it!*

To take her mind off Billy, Linda pulled Carol over to an open-air market across the way. Linda bought some fresh fruit and looked at the stalls selling locally made crafts. She picked out a pair of earrings and a bracelet. She was getting her money out of her wallet when she had that same sense of being watched again. Whirling around, she dropped her purse and the earrings and a package she was carrying for Carol. Everything went flying.

"Linda, what's gotten into you?" Carol asked,

handing her the purse. "You're acting really strange."

"It's nothing," Linda told her. "I just thought I saw someone from the boat."

"Someone? Or Billy?" Carol guessed.

Linda bit her lower lip and scanned the street. No one was there, but she couldn't get over the feeling.

He was out there.

Somewhere.

"I know it sounds weird, Carol, but I think he's been following us."

"You have really lost it," Carol said. "Come on, let's get a soda. Maybe if we sit down for a minute you'll be able to relax."

Carol found a cute sidewalk café with wrought-iron chairs and tables with umbrellas. Maybe Carol was right. Maybe Linda just needed to relax. She ordered a lemonade and settled back in her chair. Suddenly, she felt a hand come down on her shoulder.

Linda must have jumped a mile.

"Hey, girl, chill out," a familiar voice said. "What's gotten into you?"

Linda turned to see Tommy, Marla, and Kevin standing there. Tommy gave her a concerned look and asked, "Are you okay?"

"Linda's seeing things," Carol said. "She thinks Billy's been following her."

Marla's eyes went wide. "No kidding?"

"I know it sounds freaky—" Linda began.

Kevin pulled a chair out and sat on it backward, his bony elbows resting on the frame. "A tad," he agreed.

Marla nodded. "Kevin's right. Take it easy, Linda. Why would Billy be following you around?"

No reason, she said to herself.

"Anyway, if you need to talk about it, we're always here for you," Kevin added. "We're pals, right?"

"Thanks," said Linda.

Tommy smiled. A nice smile, Linda noticed for the first time. She'd never really looked carefully at Tommy before, but she saw now that he was cute. Very cute. No wonder Justine was interested in him. She decided not to hold it against Tommy that he happened to have been Billy's friend.

"Anytime," he added with a wink. "Day or night."

"Give it a rest," Marla said. "Your heart's taken, remember? I never knew how fickle Capricorns could be."

"I wish that were true," Linda answered with a laugh. "I seem to have a lot of trouble forgetting a guy once it's over!"

After an hour or so, Linda stopped thinking about Billy altogether. Eventually, Marla and Kevin headed back to the boat. Carol wanted to go back to the art gallery and buy another print. Tommy decided to wait and hang out with them.

"We can catch a cab together," he said.

The three of them left the café and headed toward the gallery. As they were walking down the crowded sidewalk, Tommy suggested they stroll in the street.

"More room this way," he said.

Tommy, Carol, and Linda strolled into the street. Linda was busy looking at the outdoor stalls. She wasn't listening for the traffic behind her.

Suddenly, Linda heard Tommy yelling at her. "Get out of the way!" he shouted.

Seconds later, a moped came barreling down the street.

"Linda!" another voice shouted.

It was Billy.

He'd appeared out of nowhere.

Linda froze. She was trapped between the

moped and Billy. There was nowhere to go.

Billy raced toward her. Linda stiffened. Billy grabbed Linda by the arms and pushed her down. He tackled her to the ground just seconds before the moped roared by—right where Linda had been standing.

CHAPTER 10

Billy really had been following her.

He sulked all the way back to the boat, and Linda could tell he was mad at her. Obviously, she wasn't grateful enough that he'd saved her life.

"I am grateful," Linda said.

I just don't think it's a reason to get back together with you.

"You think I want to see you again," Billy said. "You think that's what this is all about."

Linda looked at him in disbelief. He'd done it again!

Okay, she thought. *Maybe I'll try sending him a message. Stop reading my mind, or else!*

Billy just laughed. He and Linda were sitting in the back seat of the cab, next to Carol. Tommy was up front. They were almost at the dock, and the ship was in sight. Linda couldn't wait to get to her cabin and take a hot shower.

"You think I practically killed myself just so you'd go out with me again?" Billy nursed his right shoulder. He'd hurt it when he fell to the ground. "Billy Jackson, the big hero. Who could resist, right?"

"Something like that."

"Well, you're wrong, Linda," Billy said, huffy. "I saved you because I saw you were in danger. And I didn't want you to get hurt."

Linda wanted to believe him, but it was hard. Instead, her mind kept coming back to a truly horrifying possibility.

If Billy really had been following her, he could have set up the whole accident.

Maybe even hired the guy to run her down.

It sent a chill down her spine just thinking about it. Watching him out of the corner of her eye, she made a very firm resolution. If that was Billy's plan, it had backfired—badly.

There was no way she'd be getting back together with Billy Jackson.

Not now.

Not ever.

Later that afternoon, Linda joined Tommy, Marla, and Justine for a shuffleboard tournament. Billy sat on a deck chair nearby, his arm in a sling, and glared at them the entire time. While Marla and Kevin tried to pretend nothing was the matter, Linda felt the tension rise. Then a waiter arrived with a tray of frozen fruit drinks.

From Billy.

Linda shot Billy a look, one that Kevin noticed. "Be nice, Linda," he urged. "Maybe Billy's just trying to make up for his rotten behavior." He took a tall, frosty glass from the tray and raised it in a toast. "Thanks, chum."

"You're welcome." Billy's smile widened. But then it froze when he saw Linda refuse the drink.

"No thanks," she said, pushing the tray away.

"None for me either," Justine said.

There was an awkward pause as Tommy decided what to do. Kevin already had his drink. Marla had taken one, too, in the end. What would Tommy do?

Billy waited. So did Linda. Finally, Tommy took a glass from the tray and sipped at it, without looking at Billy.

"The guy's my friend," he explained. "There's no point in insulting him."

"I can't believe you'd take anything from him," Justine said. "Look at how he's treated Linda."

Tommy shrugged. "He keeps trying to make it

up to her. He wants to get back together. What's the problem?"

Linda didn't know what to say. In a way, Tommy was right. But Tommy and the others didn't know about the note she'd found in her cabin. Or how she suspected Billy had had her run down, just so he could look like a hero. All they knew was that Billy had a temper, and that he was angry with her about their breakup. Linda wondered again if maybe she was overreacting. Maybe there wasn't anything really wrong with Billy. Maybe he'd just made a few dumb moves.

And maybe not.

"Actually," Linda said, clearing her throat. "I've been meaning to tell you. I think Billy may have sneaked into my room the other night."

"You're kidding!" Justine cried, her big brown eyes widening.

Linda nodded. "While I was sleeping. He left me a note. And I know this sounds strange, but I have a really bad feeling about that accident in town this afternoon. I think Billy might have set it up."

Tommy moved back in his chair, obviously uncomfortable with Linda's suggestion. "That's wack, Linda. I was there. I saw that moped almost hit you. The guy was driving too fast, that was all."

"He was coming after me," said Linda.

"You think Billy hired the guy to run you down?" Marla gasped.

"That's unbelievable!" Kevin agreed.

All five of them found themselves looking Billy's way, then quickly turning their eyes away from him.

"So he could save my life," Linda confirmed.

Billy got up from his deck chair, nursing his injured arm. He strolled by their table. Everyone fell silent.

"How are the drinks?" he asked.

"Great!" Tommy said, his voice forced.

"You working out later?" Billy asked.

"Sure," said Tommy in that same tense voice.

"Okay." Billy looked at the group. There was no way Linda could tell what was going on behind those green eyes of his. "Well, see ya."

"Yeah, Billy," said Marla. "See ya later."

After he was gone, Tommy let out a long sigh. "I still think you're wrong," he said. "Billy's just upset. He wouldn't hurt you, Linda."

"Tommy's right," Justine said, trying to reassure her.

But Linda could see Justine was thinking about something, maybe even holding something back.

"What is it?" Linda asked Justine. "There's something you guys aren't telling me."

"It's nothing," Tommy said firmly.

But Justine managed to work up her nerve, despite Tommy's insistence. "It is *not* nothing. Linda, listen. Tommy doesn't want you to know about something Billy said to him. He bragged to Tommy that he hurt his last girlfriend so bad, she was never the same."

"Never the same?" Linda echoed.

"That's right." Justine nodded slowly. "The girl turned into a total wreck. Supposedly, he did some real damage."

"Damage?" Kevin asked.

"What kind of damage?" Marla's blue eyes were ringed with curiosity.

Tommy made a face and shot out of his chair. "Justine, I told you to cool it. You don't know what you're talking about. It wasn't like that."

"Oh, really?" Justine asked. Her brown eyes narrowed and focused intently on Linda. "Believe me, Linda, I've been there. Billy Jackson is trouble. Didn't anyone ever tell you? *Never* love a Libra."

CHAPTER 11

Never the same.

Did some real damage.

Hurt her so bad…

As the others talked and argued about Justine's warning, Linda took a long look at Tommy, Marla, Justine, and Kevin. They thought she was exaggerating. *It's a cruise, chill.* That was the message she kept getting. They all wanted to have fun. But what if Billy really did try to hurt her?

Would any of them come to her rescue?

Tommy? Maybe.

Marla and Kevin? Probably not.

Justine? For sure, but she wasn't exactly a football player.

No. Linda was on her own when it came to Billy. And that meant one thing.

It was time to be a resourceful Capricorn.

"I'm going to tell the captain about Billy," Linda announced to the others.

"Linda!" all four said in unison. "You can't!"

"Think about what you're doing," Tommy urged.

"Are you sure that's such a good idea?" Kevin asked. "Billy could get in a lot of trouble. Don't be rash!"

Justine was silent.

"Justine?" Linda asked.

The girl hesitated for a moment. "Are you sure it's the right thing?" she said weakly.

"You guys! Listen to what you're saying. Billy's broken the law. He *should* get in trouble."

Tommy shook his head and chewed on his lower lip. "I don't know, Linda. You still don't know for sure that Billy really tried to hurt you. Maybe we should think about it before we go ahead and blow his cover."

"I've got an idea," Kevin suggested. "Why doesn't Tommy talk to Billy? He can warn Billy that you're about to turn him in. That way, Billy will know it's serious and he'd better get with the program. Tommy can tell Billy that if he cools things down, you won't let Captain Jim know."

"That's a great idea," Marla agreed. She looked at Linda, her eyes bright. "That'll solve everything.

Billy's sure to take it easy after that."

Kevin's expression was hopeful. "Linda?"

The four of them waited for her answer.

Linda tried to see it their way.

She didn't have any proof that Billy had been in her room, or that he'd hired someone to run her down. She thought about it the way the captain would see it, and she could almost see the skeptical look in his eye.

"Maybe you guys are right," she said with a sigh. "Tonight's the Midnight Buffet. If Billy apologizes to me, then I'll keep quiet. But if I see he's up to his old tricks, I'm going to turn him in to the captain."

"We understand," Marla said, putting a protective hand on Linda's knee. "But we promise you, Linda. Billy will behave. We'll make sure of it. Right, guys?"

Linda took a long time with her hair and makeup that night. It was time to teach Billy a lesson. Maybe even be on the lookout for a cute guy. She curled her hair, then dressed in her sexiest outfit— a pale pink gown with spaghetti straps and scalloped lace around a plunging neckline. Before she left her room, she took one last look in the mirror. Her hair hung loose, practically down to her waist.

Just a touch of makeup around her eyes brought out their almond shape. A dab of lipstick, and she was ready.

Wrong.

She was devastating.

She was on her way to the dining room when she ran straight into Billy.

"Hey, Linda!" Billy said, following her. "We need to talk."

He was wearing a tuxedo and looked terrific. Briefly, Linda wondered how he'd gotten the outfit. His green eyes locked on hers. Linda felt weak in the knees. Darn it! Billy always managed to get to her.

"I'm sorry," Billy said softly.

"About what?"

"Everything. I know it'll never be like it was before," he said. "I guess I just kept hoping..." His voice trailed off. "I made the biggest mistake of my life breaking up with you, but I promise I won't keep trying to get back together. Please don't turn me in, Linda. I promise to behave." He smiled, looking almost bashful. "Please?"

Linda let out a long sigh. "Oh, all right!" she said finally. Billy really did know how to turn on the charm. "But the minute I catch you hanging around—or following me—"

Billy's eyes clouded over for a minute. "I don't know what you mean," he said.

"Like you did in town today," she added, ignoring him. "I'll turn you in, I swear I will."

"No problem," Billy said, still a bit confused. "So we've got a truce?"

"Truce," Linda reluctantly agreed.

He looked at her longingly, and for a minute, it seemed as if he was actually going to try to kiss her. Then he thought better of the idea. Instead, Billy gave Linda a small wave, and walked off with a quiet "Good-bye."

Linda watched him leave.

Could Billy really act normal?

Or had she been fooled again?

At the buffet, Billy surprised her by behaving really well. He didn't watch her or stare at her. Linda actually felt comfortable for the first time in a long time. Maybe Marla and the others had been right. Maybe Billy only needed a warning.

Billy stopped by her table once, at dessert, to set a plate of baked Alaska in front of her place.

"Peace offering," he said. "I had them make it special."

And then he was gone.

Linda shrugged and looked down at her dessert. Billy really seemed to have gotten the message.

"Gosh, Linda. That dessert looks incredible," said Carol. "Can I have a bite?"

Carol dug her fork into the dessert and ate a huge bite. "It's delicious," she said. "Why don't you try some?"

Linda eyed the dessert. She really was full. But finally she gave in. "I guess I'll have some whipped cream," she said grudgingly. She had a total soft spot for whipped cream. "You're not eating it anyway."

Linda took a bite from Carol's fork. Her cousin was right. The dessert was delicious. She had another, then propped her elbow on the table, watching Billy with Marla and the others. He looked relaxed and confident. Linda wondered again if she'd been making the whole thing up.

She took another bite of the dessert.

Suddenly, her throat tightened. She couldn't breathe. She coughed a few times, but it didn't help.

"Linda," Carol said. "Have some water. Are you okay?"

Linda gasped. "Help—" she said, choking.

She struggled for air. Spots appeared in front of her eyes and the room grew very quiet. Then, before she knew what had happened, she fell over. Everything went black before she hit the floor.

CHAPTER 12

"There was poison in the whipped cream on that baked Alaska," the voice said, speaking softly. "Not enough to kill you, just enough to warn you. If you tell anyone about me, things will start to get rough. And I'd hate to think of anything bad happening to you, Linda."

Slowly, she managed to open her eyes. A sharp pain stabbed her temple, just above her right eye. Her whole body ached, as if she had come down with a wicked flu.

"Where am I?" she asked. The bed where she lay had metal rails, and there was a smell of antiseptic in the air.

"They put you in the infirmary," Billy told her. "They're pretty sure you've got the flu."

Linda couldn't believe how smug he sounded.

95

Obviously, Billy thought he was going to get away with this.

"What about Carol?"

"She didn't have any whipped cream."

Linda's stomach curled in on itself. That was Carol, trying to avoid the extra calories. And there was Linda, plowing into the whipped cream.

She couldn't bring herself to look at Billy.

The very thought of him terrified her.

"I'll get you for this, Billy," she said weakly. "I'll tell the captain and he'll put you off the boat in Fort Lauderdale."

"Unfortunately for you, Linda, that's impossible. We left Fort Lauderdale a few hours ago. We'll be at sea until we reach Ocho Rios."

The wail inside Linda's head drowned out Billy's voice.

They'd left port, and Billy was still onboard.

Her nightmare was only just beginning.

Billy got up to leave. Linda heard the door close, and she knew she was alone.

Completely, absolutely, utterly alone.

One by one, they all came to visit. Tommy. Justine. Marla. Kevin. Carol. Captain Jim.

Every time another visitor showed up, Linda was ready to tell them that Billy had poisoned her.

But Billy was always there. Whenever Linda had company, Billy appeared.

As if he knew.

Linda had always wondered about Billy's psychic sense. When they were together, he seemed able to read her mind. Now it was as if he knew she was waiting for the chance to tell someone about him. And he made sure there was no way she could.

She went to use the phone in the infirmary.

Billy showed up at the door, shaking his finger.

All that night and all the next day, he was there. Guarding her. Watching her.

When Carol came to visit, Billy showed up.

Linda thought she was going crazy.

Billy fed her the food the nurse brought. He read to her. He changed the channel on the television. She had no one to talk to but him, no way to explain how she was feeling. But she knew that at some point, Billy would slip up. He'd miss being there. And she would escape. She'd be free.

She'd find a way to tell them exactly what Billy Jackson was up to.

After a day and a half in the infirmary, Linda was well enough to go back to her room. Billy stood guard there, too. But the next morning, Linda found herself alone—Carol had gone off to visit Captain Jim on the bridge and Billy was standing guard outside the door. Linda finally managed to think of a plan for getting away from Billy.

First she unplugged her phone.

Then she took a very long—and very hot—bath.

While she was still wet, she crawled into bed and started to moan.

"Billy," she called out. "Something's wrong. Come quick!"

Billy let himself into her cabin. "Linda!" he said. "What's going on? You look terrible."

"I don't know," Linda moaned. "I think I'm having a relapse. Is that possible with poison?"

"I don't know." Billy looked her over, obviously worried. "I'll call the nurse. Maybe she can help."

"The phone's not working," Linda said weakly. "I already tried. Maybe you should go down there. I can't believe how bad I feel. I think I'm going to die!"

"Don't say that!" Billy checked Linda's forehead, which was still burning up. Once he was convinced she wasn't faking, he got even more upset. "Are you sure you'll be okay?" he asked.

"I think so," Linda told him. "Hurry!"

A second after Billy left, Linda plugged the phone back in and dialed the captain's office. It seemed to ring a thousand times. Finally, Captain Jim answered.

"Captain Stamatakos, it's Linda Sellers. Listen, I don't have much time," Linda said, the words coming out in a rush. "Billy Jackson's the stowaway. If you come here right away, you might be able to catch him in my cabin. Hurry, please!"

Ten minutes later, Billy still hadn't come back. Carol was there, along with Captain Jim. Linda told them the whole story, including Billy's confession that he'd poisoned her.

"I'll have him arrested right away," Jim said to Linda. "We'll put him ashore when we get to Ocho Rios and turn him over to the authorities."

"What will happen to him?" Linda asked.

"Chances are he'll be extradited to Florida," Captain Jim told her. "He'll be tried there. That young man's facing some serious charges—"

The door opened a crack while Jim was speaking.

"Billy!"

Then it slammed shut.

"He heard you!" Linda said, panicking. "He's getting away!"

Jim, Carol, and Linda raced from the room. But there was no sign of Billy anywhere. Not in the hall. Not out on the deck near Linda's cabin.

"Don't worry," Jim told her. "I'll have the crew search every inch of this ship. There's no way Billy Jackson can get off this boat. We'll find him, Linda. I promise."

They didn't. Billy had hiding places all over the boat. And he was using them. The crew knew the ship, but Billy seemed to know it better.

For Linda, it was worse than a nightmare. She couldn't sleep. She couldn't eat. All she could think of was that Billy was out there.

Somewhere.

And now he was angry.

There was only one person who could really help, Linda realized, and that was Tommy.

Since the day Linda had told Captain Jim about Billy, Tommy, Marla, Justine, and Kevin had all avoided her. It wasn't that they were mean to her or anything. They just weren't into hanging out anymore. Even so, there was still a chance that Tommy might be willing to help her. Maybe she could convince him that it would be better for Billy if he turned himself in.

Linda called Tommy at the gym. The girl who answered the phone told Linda that Tommy was busy, but he'd be free when his shift ended at ten. Linda left a message asking him to meet her on the deck afterward.

Ten o'clock came and went. Finally, at ten-thirty Tommy showed up, apologetic and just a little nervous.

"Billy came by the gym right as I was getting off," he explained. "The guy looks like he's been sleeping in a garbage pail. He's pretty wrecked, Linda."

"I'm sure he is," said Linda. "But he tried to kill me, Tommy! Doesn't that count for anything?"

Tommy chewed on his lip and looked over his shoulder. Linda was standing with her back to the rail, and glanced past Tommy. "Do you think he followed you?" she asked, trying to see if anything moved on the deck behind him.

"I don't know," Tommy said. He jammed his hands in his pockets. "What do you want me to do?" he asked.

"Try to reason with him," Linda said. "There's no point in his hiding out. Eventually, they're going to find him. He's got to realize that."

"I think he's got other plans," said Tommy.

"Not the mutiny?"

Tommy nodded. "He's already got Captain Jim's gun."

Linda drew in a sharp breath. Billy was becoming more dangerous by the minute. Now the whole ship had reason to worry. "What'll he do?"

"Who knows?" Tommy said. He moved closer to Linda, who stood with her back to the rail. "I have to admit, Linda, I'm actually afraid. Billy's lost it." Tommy put his hands on Linda's shoulders and rubbed them gently. "I want to help you, but I don't know if I can stop him."

The touch of Tommy's warm hands felt good.

Tommy leaned closer, and Linda could feel his breath on her cheek. Then his soft lips were coming down on hers in a kiss.

Maybe I should have resisted, Linda thought later.

Maybe I could have saved Tommy's life.

The kiss was just ending when Linda saw the oar. It came down out of the darkness, a blur of white against the black night.

CHAPTER 13

There was an awful crack as the oar made contact.

Tommy slumped to the ground, unconscious.

And Billy stepped forward.

"You see, Linda," Billy demanded, his eyes ablaze. "You see what you've done? You asked him to help you. That was a big mistake."

On the deck, Tommy moaned softly. Billy planted his foot on Tommy's back. From the scary, distant look in Billy's eyes, Linda knew she'd made a big mistake. She backed away from Billy. She had to find the captain.

"I don't think so," said Billy. In his hand, a steel object glinted.

The captain's gun.

"You're not going anywhere, Linda," Billy said. "Unless it's with me."

He reached out for Linda's arm. But Linda stepped out of his grasp.

And then she ran.

She'd surprised Billy, so she had a head start. She raced down the deck as fast as she could.

"You won't get away, Linda," she heard Billy calling out behind her. "I'll catch you."

A shot rang out.

Linda ducked.

The shot ricocheted off the railing on her left. Linda darted to her right, her heart pounding. She pushed through a nearby door, then turned to glance over her shoulder. Billy's face appeared in the door's glass window. His eyes were wild and a sickening grin crossed his face. Then he yanked on the door, pulling it open.

Linda screamed.

She tore off down the hall, with no idea where she was headed. She took a left, then a right, then she was racing for another door at the end of the hallway. She pushed on through the door, and found herself standing at the bow of the boat. From here, there was nowhere to go.

Nowhere but down.

For a minute, Linda actually thought about diving overboard. Was that the only way to escape Billy Jackson?

Another shot rang out, shattering the night.

Linda darted to her right. She took cover behind a cluster of deck chairs.

Another shot. Farther away this time.

Billy had lost her trail.

Linda cowered even deeper behind the deck chairs. She could hear Billy stomping around on the deck. Her heart raced. His footsteps seemed to be getting farther away. They made their way around the other side of the deck, around the back of the ship from where Linda was hiding. But then they came back again. Billy seemed to know Linda was there, but he couldn't spot her.

She was trapped.

Or maybe not.

Linda saw she was directly across the deck from a row of lifeboats covered by heavy canvas tarps. There was a high wall between the deck and the boats, but if she could manage to get under a tarp without Billy seeing her, then it would make a good hiding place. Maybe she'd actually be able to convince Billy that he'd lost her. It was worth a shot.

It was her only shot.

She waited for Billy's footsteps to recede. Then she made a dash for the lifeboat. She didn't look to see if Billy was there, watching her. She just threw herself over the wall and into the nearest boat. She ripped off the tarp and climbed in.

Her heart was racing a mile a minute.

She pulled the tarp back over the boat.

And held her breath.

If Billy had seen her, she'd know soon enough.

Seconds passed, then minutes. To Linda, it felt like a lifetime. She huddled in the bottom of the boat and listened for some sign that Billy had seen her.

"I know you're out here, Linda," came Billy's voice. "And believe me, I'm going to find you."

His footsteps came so close, Linda thought Billy must know where she was hiding. But then they grew fainter again. She could hear him pacing up and down the deck, frantically searching for her.

"You can't fool me, Linda," he said. "I know you're here. You're a part of me."

Linda bit her lip so hard she drew blood. Could he really read her mind? Could he use that psychic link to tell where she was hiding?

Impossible, her logical Capricorn instincts told her.

Or not? the mystical side of her wondered.

Suddenly, she felt the lifeboat jolt alive beneath

her. Then she heard the screeching sound of a pulley going to work.

The boat started to rise.

"Guess what, Linda?" Billy's voice called out. "Looks like you're going for a ride."

Linda swept the tarp off her. Frantic, she glanced over the edge of the boat. She was high up in the air. The deck looked very far away.

Billy was busy pulling a rope at the side of the boat. "You know what, Linda? I think you were right after all. It just isn't working out. Besides, you saw what I did to Tommy. That makes you a witness—"

"A witness to what?" Linda's voice came out a shriek. Below her, the icy waters of the ocean churned. "Tommy's still alive," she said. "I saw him move."

"He *was* alive."

Billy lowered the boat. When it dropped to eye level, Linda met Billy's gaze. The look he gave her was chilling.

Hurt her so bad.

Never the same.

Billy had done this before.

Maybe not this exact same way, but there had been a girl. A very unfortunate girl.

Billy let go of the rope.

The boat plummeted down to the dark ocean below.

The jolt rammed Linda's chest into her throat. She fell to her knees. Looking up, she saw Billy waving to her, his final good-bye.

And then she saw him lift a body and hurl it overboard.

CHAPTER 14

It landed with a giant splash.

Tommy.

Linda's shouts echoed in the dark night.

But the ship cruised on. No one heard her. No one came on deck.

She was alone.

She grabbed onto the oars in the lifeboat, and, trembling, crying, rowed for her life.

Tommy's body sank, and Linda rowed on.

After a while, she stopped crying. After a while, she became numb. She couldn't feel her hands or the blisters there. She couldn't feel her aching arms and shoulders. She couldn't feel her fear, except for the brief moments when it overcame her and held her tight.

She rowed for what felt like hours, shouting

for help as loud as she could. Her voice became hoarse, her throat raw.

She'd almost given up hope when she looked up at the ship and spotted someone on deck.

"Help!" she cried. "Help me!"

"Who's out there?" a voice demanded. A person leaned over the rail.

"I'm a passenger from the ship," she cried. "Get the captain!"

Linda nearly cried in relief when she saw the figure disappear from the rail. Linda used her last ounce of energy to row the lifeboat alongside the ship. Then someone let down a rope ladder, and Linda climbed back onboard, her arms burning from the effort.

Carol was there, along with Captain Jim. Her cousin rushed over to give Linda a hug.

"What happened?" she asked breathlessly. "We looked for you everywhere. We stopped the ship, we were so worried. What on earth were you doing *overboard,* in a *lifeboat?*"

"Billy threw me over," Linda said, breaking down at last. "He…Tommy…" She realized that for the past hour, she'd been trying to forget the awful sight of Tommy's body being hurled overboard. But now she had to face it.

"Tommy's dead," she said. "Billy killed him."

Captain Jim and Carol were dumbstruck. But the captain soon rushed into action. He ordered the entire crew awakened. "We're going to find this criminal," he said, "once and for all."

This time, they succeeded.

They found Billy lurking in a spot belowdecks, not far from where he'd given Linda the tour. Linda saw him taken away with her own eyes. And she had the captain's promise that nothing would prevent him from putting Billy ashore at Ocho Rios, the very next day.

As for Tommy, they searched the waters, but with no success. His body had disappeared into the deep, dark sea.

Since they couldn't find Tommy's body, the captain told Linda there was a chance Billy might not even be prosecuted. It was his word against Linda's, and there wasn't another witness.

Linda couldn't believe it.

Billy was going to get away, scot-free.

At breakfast the next morning, Linda exploded. "I saw Tommy fall. I saw the oar come down right on top of his—"

"Linda," Justine whispered. "Please stop talking about it. I don't know how much more I can take."

Justine's face was white and her eyes were red from crying. When she'd heard the news about Tommy, Justine had broken down in tears. She'd barely stopped crying since. Now she played with the food in front of her, unable to eat anything.

Linda immediately felt bad. "I'm sorry," she said. "I'll stop talking about it."

"I'm not sure we should," Marla said. "Justine needs to deal with her anger."

"My anger?" Justine asked in disbelief. "What are you talking about?"

"You must be mad at Billy," said Marla. "He killed Tommy."

"I realize that," Justine snapped. "But I'm not angry. I'm upset. Tommy's dead and I'm upset. That's all!"

Justine stood up and stormed away. Marla looked at Linda and raised an eyebrow. "She's in denial," she said. "Wouldn't you be stark raving mad at Billy Jackson if he killed your boyfriend?"

"Right now, I'm mostly just afraid. As far as I'm concerned, we can't get him off this boat soon enough." To Linda, it was beginning to feel as if Billy really did control the ship—just the way he'd always wanted.

At nine in the morning, Captain Jim personally escorted Billy from the cabin where he'd been held under watch. Justine, Linda, Marla, and Kevin watched from the deck as the captain led Billy down the ramp and handed him over to the local police.

Billy gazed up at them, standing at the rail. Despite the warm day, Linda felt a shiver as Billy's intense green gaze met hers. Despite everything that had happened, she felt a tug of regret.

Would he call out to her?

But Billy turned away, strangely silent. Justine was quiet, the same way she'd been ever since Tommy died. Marla put an arm around Linda's shoulder. Kevin just sighed.

"He's gone, Linda," Marla said. "Out of your life. Forever."

For some reason, Linda wasn't convinced.

Linda sunbathed. She swam. She had the vacation she should have had all along. She went ashore with Carol and ate dinner with Justine and Marla and Kevin. The group chatted and gossiped and tried not to talk about what had happened.

It should have been perfect.

Except...

Linda felt as if Billy Jackson was still on the ship.

Sure, she'd seen him walk off the boat. As far as she could tell, he was *gone*.

It just didn't feel that way.

Maybe Billy was just a nightmare she couldn't forget.

The truth was, she kept imagining things.

Seeing things.

Hearing things.

Like Billy's voice in her ear at the movies. Or Billy's footsteps following her on the deck. Billy's smile in the mirror—instead of her own reflection—when she went to brush her teeth at night.

Playing shuffleboard with Marla and Justine and Kevin, Linda heard a voice in her ear.

"You're my partner—or no one's," he said.

She turned around.

Billy was gone.

At dinner, she felt someone at her elbow.

"Care to order dessert?" Billy's voice asked. "The whipped cream's fresh…"

When she looked up, the waiter was looking at her, a strange expression on his face.

When she browsed in the boutique, Billy's voice whispered to her, soft and low, "Let me buy you something—maybe a ring?"

She was going crazy.

That was one explanation.

On the deck at night, there was Billy, whispering to her. When she turned around, no one was there.

At breakfast, Billy's voice in her ear, telling her what to order.

Linda moved to another table.

In the movies, Billy's laugh in her ear.

Linda left the theater, her heart racing.

It's all in my head, she told herself.

"Sure it is," Billy replied.

I'm going crazy.

"You bet your life," Billy shot back.

Finally, when she couldn't take it anymore, Linda decided to say something to Justine and the others. Late in the afternoon, the three girls and Kevin were lounging on the deck, taking in the sun. That day, the ship had docked at Grand Cayman. Now they'd left port and were heading toward Cozumel. After that, it was on to Key West—and then home. Only four more days left in their cruise.

Four more days of torture, if Billy didn't leave her alone.

Billy's gone, Sellers, she told herself. *You're torturing yourself.*

Marla and Kevin were playing backgammon, chatting away as usual. Justine had her nose—and her thoughts—buried in a magazine. "Anybody want a cold drink?" she asked, getting up from her deck chair.

"I'm fine," said Linda. "Nothing for me, thanks."

"Marla? Kevin?"

"No thanks. You want company?"

Justine focused her eyes on Marla. The look came from a distance. Ever since Tommy had died, Justine wasn't the same. Of course, no one expected her to be her usual bubbly self, but even Linda noticed how out of it Justine was acting. She picked at her food and didn't pay attention—even when someone was talking right to her. Now Justine didn't even answer Marla. Instead, she just shrugged and walked away.

"Do you think she's okay?" Linda asked. "I mean, maybe we should try to get her some help."

"The girl's had quite a shock," Kevin added. "We can't expect her to be totally over it right away."

"I guess you're right." Linda pulled her chair closer to Marla and Kevin. "Guys, I know it sounds crazy," she said in a low voice. "But this creepy thing keeps happening to me."

"What?" Marla asked, her blue eyes serious.

"I keep hearing Billy's voice," Linda confessed. She was really relieved to be finally talking about it. "Do you think it's possible Billy didn't get off the boat?"

Kevin frowned and looked at Marla. "Linda, we saw him leave. Captain Jim took him away."

"I know," said Linda. "But I've been getting these weird feelings lately, like he's still here. And this morning, when I woke up? I thought I heard him outside my door."

"That's so bizarre, Linda," Marla said, shivering noticeably. "You know what I think?"

"What?" Linda asked.

"I think you need a vacation from your vacation." Marla forced a laugh. "Seriously. Didn't you win that day of beauty for turning Billy in?"

Linda nodded. The captain had given Linda a certificate to spend the day in the ship's spa.

"Have you used it yet?" Marla asked.

"No."

"Well, it's time, girl," said Kevin. "You sound as if you could use it."

Linda gazed at them both. A flicker of worry passed over Marla's big blue eyes. Kevin's smile seemed forced. Was it her imagination, or did they seem almost scared? Billy had killed Tommy and nearly tried to kill Linda. If Linda was right, and Billy really still was aboard, there was every reason for them all to be afraid.

"Captain Jim turned Billy over to the police," Kevin stated flatly. The look of fear was gone, replaced by a confident expression. "It's over."

Justine came back with a soda and sipped it without saying a word. Marla sat with her back to the rail, silent behind her dark sunglasses. Kevin absently rolled the dice on the backgammon set.

Billy was gone.

Tommy was dead.

It was just the four of them now. If they stuck together, maybe they'd be safe. But Linda had a funny feeling, looking over at Justine and Marla and Kevin. If they really were still in danger, she'd be on her own.

Linda took Marla and Kevin's advice. The very next day, she signed up for a full spa treatment. She had a massage, a facial, and a mud wrap. By lunchtime, she decided that Marla was right. All the pampering really did take her mind off Billy. After lunch, she was off to the sauna for some serious, deep-pore cleansing.

The sauna was empty when Linda let herself in. She lay down on the rough cedar bench, breathing in the hot, fragrant air. The rocks were blazing and the heat felt great.

Ever since the night Tommy died, Linda hadn't slept very well. Now, after her massage, she finally felt relaxed. The heat from the sauna made her even drowsier, and pretty soon, she was dozing off.

She woke with a jolt. From the clock on the wall, she saw that no more than ten minutes had passed. More than enough time to clear out her pores.

Linda gathered her towel and her water bottle. She pushed on the handle of the sauna.

It wouldn't budge. Linda tried again. She was locked in. Then she heard an awful voice, deadly familiar, calling to her from the other side.

"Now you're *my* prisoner, Linda. How does it feel to have the scales turn against you?"

CHAPTER 15

Linda backed away from the door.

She *was* imagining it.

Billy couldn't possibly be out there.

"Of course I am," he shouted. "And I'm not going away! I loved you, Linda. But you let me down. No one lets me down! *Ever!*"

Billy let out a long, sick laugh.

"Ever heard of the game cat and mouse? Well, I'm the cat, and you're the mouse. Meow!"

She heard his footsteps and knew he had left. Then she pushed on the door. A blast of fresh, cool air greeted her. Linda took several deep breaths and raced out of the locker room. But the hallway outside was empty, and Linda's suspicions were confirmed.

Billy was gone.

I'm the cat, and you're the mouse.

Linda shivered.

Billy was insane.

And he was after her.

She dressed in a hurry, then headed back to her cabin. Carol was there, getting ready for dinner. She took one look at her cousin, sat her down on the bed, and made her tell her what happened.

"Billy's back on the ship," Linda said. "I heard him outside the sauna."

"What?" Carol's eyes widened. "I can't believe it! Captain Jim handed him over to the police in Ocho Rios."

"Well, he got away," said Linda. "He's been following me, Carol. It's the creepiest thing. I've heard him whispering to me, asking me questions. Whenever I turn around, he's gone. But this time, I saw him! He was outside the sauna. He locked me in. He was laughing at me! Then he left, and I managed to get out. But when I looked for him, he was gone."

"Whoa." Carol made Linda look at her. "Slow down there, kiddo. You've heard him, but then he isn't there? You saw him, then he disappeared? Are you sure you're feeling okay?"

Carol's expression told Linda the truth. Her cousin didn't completely believe her. "Tell you what," said Carol. "Why don't we head to the dining room? A little food might just clear your head."

"No way," said Linda. She planted herself on the small couch and folded her arms. "I'm staying right here—where it's safe."

From then on, Linda stayed in her cabin. She had no desire to be out in public and have Billy Jackson stalking her. Justine and Marla and Kevin all thought she was crazy. Carol probably did, too, but she wouldn't tell Linda that to her face. Even though she had to bring food back to the cabin after every meal.

Linda didn't care. She counted off the days until the ship docked back in Fort Lauderdale.

Three more days and she'd be free again.

They all think I'm nuts, but I know what I saw. Billy locked me in that sauna. He's out there, I just know it.

From her porthole, Linda could see the wide, blue sea. The ship had left Cozumel the day before. Now they were on their way east to Key West. On the surface, everything seemed so innocent. Through her cabin door, Linda heard the sounds of the passengers, talking, laughing, shouting to one another. So happy, as if they didn't have a care in the world.

And they didn't.

But she did.

Because once upon a time, she'd made the big mistake of falling in love—with a Libra.

As long as she stayed in her room, Linda didn't hear Billy's taunting voice, and she wasn't afraid. She paced the floor, and she read. She wrote in her diary, trying to make sense of what had happened.

I know I should have thought more about Billy from the start. He was so overwhelming, so intense. I liked that. I hope that the next time I fall in love—and it won't be very soon, that's for sure—I can keep my head about me. They say that's a Capricorn's biggest fault: impulsiveness. I want to be less impulsive! I know I shouldn't blame myself too much, but when I look back, I realize that I just didn't think, I didn't see the warning signs.

What warning signs?

Were there ever warning signs that told you a guy would go overboard?

Totally off the deep end?

After two days holed up in her cabin, Linda started to jump at every sound. Finally, Carol dragged Linda to the mirror and showed her just how unhealthy she looked.

There were dark circles around her eyes. Her cheeks were sunken. Her lips were chapped and cracked from licking them nervously.

"You've got to leave this room." Carol held Linda by the shoulders, giving her a long, sisterly stare. "Today. Now. Promise me you will."

"I promise," Linda agreed. "But what if Billy sees me?"

"Billy isn't out there," Carol said. "He's gone, Linda. Honestly. Captain Jim has searched the ship three times, just to make sure. There's no sign of him. You've got to believe us, we're not lying to you."

"You think I'm imagining things," Linda said weakly.

"I know you are," said Carol. "Now come on. I want to see you pack some things. A bathing suit, some suntan lotion, a towel. And I want to see you on deck in an hour."

"What if I swim in the indoor pool?" Linda asked. She knew she sounded like a complete idiot, but she didn't want to be outside, where Billy could easily spot her.

Billy was gone.

That's what they all said.

But Linda still didn't believe them.

Carol wasn't crazy about the idea, but finally nodded her head in agreement. "Okay. The underground pool. Why don't you call Justine or Marla and see if they'll go with you? Maybe you'd feel better if you hung out with your friends."

Linda picked up the phone and called Justine. She was happy to go along with Linda, and agreed to meet her by the pool in half an hour.

"Satisfied?" Linda asked her cousin after she'd hung up.

Carol nodded. "Very. How about meeting me for a soda afterward? We can play shuffleboard before dinner."

"Sure."

Carol left the cabin and Linda gathered up her things. When she couldn't justify waiting any longer, she eased the cabin door open, peered into the hall, and stepped outside.

No Billy.

She headed down the hall and made a turn toward the stairs. For a brief moment, she thought about turning back.

He's not on the ship, she told herself. *Why can't you believe them when they say that?*

Because she couldn't. But there was no way she could prove them wrong either.

To reach the pool, Linda took several flights of stairs to a lower deck. Then she walked down a series of long corridors. On either side of the hallway were several of the same metal hatches Billy had pointed out to her on that first tour.

Justine was waiting for Linda by the pool. She gave her a big hug and a smile. "I'm glad to see you left your room. We were worried there that you'd never make it out alive."

Linda smiled back. Maybe she was being ridiculous. It sure did feel good to leave the cabin.

She lowered herself into the pool and swam a few easy laps. Then she picked up her speed, glad to be getting the exercise. The water was warm, the echo of voices off the tile was comforting. Linda could almost imagine she was safe.

As she swam, she listened for Billy's voice. But it was gone. There was just her and the water and Justine, keeping up with her, lap for lap.

The girls swam for half an hour, then rested for a while. "You're giving me a real workout," said Justine, panting heavily. "I guess you needed to blow off some serious steam, huh?"

"I guess so," said Linda. Finally, she felt relaxed. She hadn't looked over her shoulder in at least twenty minutes. And her stomach was rumbling. She almost laughed.

"What's so funny?" Justine asked.

"I'm hungry," said Linda. "For the first time in days, I actually have an appetite."

"Sure you're hungry," said Justine. "It's almost dinnertime!"

Linda climbed out of the pool and toweled herself off. There was still enough time to shower and change before she was supposed to meet Carol. She gathered her things and said good-bye.

"See you later," Linda said to Justine. "And thanks for the company. I guess I really did need it."

"I'll say," said Justine. "You look about fifty times better."

More like a million, Linda realized as she headed away from the pool and back to the stairs. She thought of how she'd wasted all that time, worrying about Billy. Talk about stupid!

"You bet you were stupid," came a voice. "Stupid not to trust your instincts. *Ha ha ha ha ha ha!*"

Billy!

He was back!

Linda raced on, her hands covering her ears.

"Stop!" she shouted. "Leave me alone!"

"Never!" came Billy's voice.

The harder Linda ran, the louder the laughter grew. She raced for the stairs, but they were still at least a hundred feet away.

Hurry! Linda told herself.

The footsteps were right behind her.

The laughter went on and on.

Then Linda heard an explosion behind her. One of the metal hatches flew open, and gallons of seawater poured into the ship.

CHAPTER 16

⚖

The water gushed along the hall, pushing Linda toward the stairs. She lost her footing and fell, and the water sucked her under.

Linda flailed, swallowing big lungfuls of water. She reached out, hoping to grab on to something.

It was no use.

The water flung her against the staircase. And then it started to rise. Linda dog-paddled toward the stairs. Finally, she was able to grab on to the railing and hoist herself up.

Once she was at the top of the stairs, Linda looked down. The entire hallway was flooded with water—all the way up to the ceiling.

Beyond the water—somewhere—was Billy Jackson.

Still laughing.

Still running the show.

This time, Linda vowed, she was going to get even.

Up until now, she'd been letting the Libra have all the fun. But Linda was a competitive Capricorn, and it was time to show her stuff.

If Billy wanted a showdown, then that was exactly what he was going to get.

"Events bring you closer to your goal," read Linda's horoscope the next morning. *"The end is within reach. Focus on organization, ability to bring order out of chaos. Love relationship is tenuous, but ultimately durable."*

Ha, Linda thought, slamming the astro-diary shut. *Try unendurable!*

It was the last day of the cruise. Tomorrow, they'd be heading into Fort Lauderdale.

That meant it was also Linda's last chance. She had exactly twenty-four hours to hunt down Billy Jackson—and make him pay.

She hadn't told anyone about the accident with the hatch. No one would believe her anyway. Justine had still been at the pool when the hatch opened, but she hadn't seen Billy.

And Billy knew what he was doing, too. The water only flooded that corridor. He'd closed off the door to the pool. Linda really had been trapped. If it hadn't been for the stairs, she would have drowned.

But she was through feeling scared.

Now she was mad.

She was going to bring Billy Jackson in, and watch him confess—in front of everyone—what he'd done.

Linda dressed in a T-shirt and shorts. After a quick breakfast, she spent the whole morning searching the boat. She checked the area below-decks that Billy had shown her. She hunted around the gym. She looked for Billy's things in the closet where Tommy had hidden him. She even got a map of all the areas belowdecks, and wandered through each and every corridor.

No luck.

By the end of the day, Linda was almost ready to give up. She stopped by the promenade deck, where Marla, Justine, and Kevin were taking in the last rays of sun.

"I can't believe the cruise is ending tomorrow," Marla said.

"Me neither," said Linda, flopping into the deck chair next to Justine.

"You sound disappointed," Marla said. "I'd think you'd be happy to get off the boat." She winked at Kevin. "Because of Billy, I mean."

"Not exactly," said Linda. She stared into the girl's cold blue eyes. "I'm sure he's on this boat, Marla, and I'm going to search all night if I have to."

Marla frowned, but for some reason, Kevin smiled slightly. "Should we tell her?" he asked. "Don't you think it's time she found out?"

"Found out what?" Linda asked, totally confused.

"Actually, Linda, Billy *is* on the boat," Marla confessed. "Kevin and I helped him get back onboard."

Linda couldn't believe her ears. "What?" she asked, stunned. "Did you know about this, Justine?"

Justine sank low in her deck chair. She wouldn't meet Linda's eye. "Only afterward," she admitted. "I promised I'd keep it a secret."

"But I don't understand," Linda cried. The news was still sinking in. "How could you do this to me?"

Kevin bit his lip. "Honestly, there's a very simple answer. Billy asked us to help him out. I went ashore in Ocho Rios to take him his things. He convinced me to spring him, and I did."

"It was that simple," Linda said.

"I suppose," Kevin admitted. "We never thought—"

"That he was a maniac," Linda snapped. "Well, he is. I hope you all feel worse than rotten about what you've done." Linda looked at Marla, Kevin, and Justine in disbelief. They acted as if they'd been playing a big game—and the pawns were Linda and Billy. But it was a lot more serious than that. Billy had killed someone, and now he was after her.

Kevin leaned toward Linda and put a hand on her knee. "What harm did we do, really?"

"What harm!" Linda exploded. "Billy is trying to *kill* me, that's the harm! He's been after me, and you knew all along. You told me I was crazy, and you knew I wasn't!"

"Sorry." Marla leaned back and replaced her sunglasses. "We made a mistake."

"You sure did!" Linda practically screamed. "He killed Tommy, and you were just going to let him wander around the boat like nothing happened."

Marla's expression remained calm. Linda felt like smacking her. Instead, she drew a deep breath, trying to get her head on straight. If Kevin let Billy back on, then Kevin must be hiding him, too.

Linda stood up.

"Where are you going?" Marla asked.

"To find him."

None of them stopped her.

Five minutes later, Linda was standing outside Kevin's cabin. She rapped on the door several times, but there wasn't any answer. Finally, she reached into her purse for a piece of paper and a pen.

Dinner at eight. Don't be late. Love, Linda.

There were candles burning on the small table in Linda's stateroom. She'd ordered two plates of food, flowers, and champagne from room service. Then she dressed in her sexiest outfit: the same floor-length, pale pink gown she'd worn to the Midnight Buffet, when Billy had poisoned her. Somehow, it seemed fitting. She wouldn't be serving poisoned food to Billy, but if all went well, this would be the end.

While she put on her makeup, Linda could barely control her shaking hands. She still was in shock about what Kevin and the others had done. They thought it was a game. Would they think any differently now that the game had turned deadly?

Now wasn't the time to be preoccupied, Linda told herself. In five minutes, Billy Jackson would be stepping through the door to her suite.

Or would he?

If he came, Linda was ready for him.

She took a long, last look in the mirror. The dress showed off her pale skin and red hair. She'd let her hair down tonight, and it cascaded past her shoulders in soft, thick curls.

Yes, she said to her reflection. *You're ready.*

The question is, is he?

The bell rang at eight on the dot. Linda's stomach lurched. Was it possible that she really was about to trap Billy Jackson?

"Hello, Linda."

Billy was dressed in a tuxedo. His hair was neatly combed and fell in long curls to his neck. Face-to-face with Billy again, Linda practically lost her voice.

"Can I come in?" he asked.

"Of course."

Calm, Linda told herself. *Cool. Collected. Lure him into your trap.*

Then spring it.

"You know I'm sorry about what happened," Billy said as he made his way into the room. "I never meant for things to get so out of control."

Get him sitting, relaxed.

He'll never know what hit him.

"Let's not talk about that," she said sweetly. "Hungry?"

"Not for food."

He moved a few steps closer to Linda, who squirmed out of his reach.

"Later. Dinner's ready. We don't want it to get cold, do we?"

She seated Billy away from the door. That would make his escape harder.

"I knew Marla and Kevin had the right idea," Billy said. He placed a napkin in his lap. "You see? We really do belong together."

Billy leaned back in his chair, relaxed and smiling. Linda could hardly believe he could be so calm, so unconcerned. She'd actually seen him murder someone! And he didn't seem to be worried, not one bit.

Linda swallowed the fear that rose up in her. Now was not the time to lose her cool.

She uncovered his food.

Billy bent over the plate.

His face went white.

"What's the matter, Billy?" Linda asked. "Don't you like what's on the menu?"

A hundred cockroaches squirmed on his plate.

While Billy was busy watching them, Linda grabbed the rope she'd planted in the nearby desk. She was on him in a second, holding his hands behind his back and tying them to the chair.

"Linda!" Billy squirmed. "Cut it out! What's going on?"

"What's going on," Linda said through gritted teeth, "is that I'm putting you away, once and for all."

Now that Billy's hands were tied, Linda used another length of rope to secure his legs to the chair. After that, she rushed to the door of the cabin, taking her key with her.

"Sayonara, Billy," Linda said.

And then she slammed the door in his face.

Linda raced to the bridge. Captain Jim was there, along with Carol. She caught them in the middle of a tight embrace.

Carol stepped out of Jim's arms, red-faced and embarrassed. "What is it, Linda?" she asked, rearranging her dress.

"It's Billy!" Linda was panting from her run. "He's in my room! I caught him."

"Billy Jackson?" Captain Jim said in disbelief. "But we took him off the boat."

"Marla and Kevin let him back on," Linda explained.

Carol's eyes went wide. "I can't believe it. You were right this whole time."

"You bet I was," said Linda. "But there isn't any time to waste. I want to see him locked up—tonight!"

Jim, Carol, and Linda rushed back down to her cabin. Linda's hands were shaking as she put the key in the lock. Her plan had worked! She really was about to put Billy away for good.

She threw open the door with a flourish. The candles were still burning, the food was still on the table. Everything was exactly as she had left it.

Except for one crucial detail.

Billy Jackson was gone.

CHAPTER 17

Linda rushed into the room, frantic. "I tied him up to this chair," she insisted. "He must have gotten free."

But how?

The room was locked.

But the porthole was open.

Linda looked out the large, rectangular window. Billy must have used it to escape. He'd crawled out the window, jumped onto the deck below, and was gone.

"Tied him up with what?" Jim asked.

Linda searched the floor under the table. The ropes were gone, too. She stood up and looked at the situation through the captain's eyes. A table for two, cockroaches still wandering over the food. Candlelight. A guest who was escorted off the boat days ago, while everyone watched.

Captain Jim coughed quietly. "Well. If Billy happens to come back, you'll let me know, of course. Carol?"

Carol was caught between her cousin and Jim, obviously unsure of what to do. "You know we want to believe you," she said finally. "Do you want to hang out with us for a while?"

"Maybe later," Linda said weakly.

Carol and Jim left and as she closed the door behind them, Linda felt a wave of despair wash over her. No one believed her. No one was willing to think that Billy was out there—somewhere.

Come on, Sellers, she told herself. *Where's that Capricorn tenacity? Don't just stand here and cry. Go out there—and get him.*

Linda prowled the decks. She went slowly and listened carefully. If Billy was out here, then he was probably stalking her, too.

After searching for at least an hour, she stopped on the sports deck and leaned over the rail. Suddenly, she knew she wasn't alone. She spun around.

Behind her were a row of portholes, the windows of the penthouse staterooms. Was that a glimpse of Billy she'd caught in one of the windows?

Linda stood and looked for several minutes, but nothing moved. She turned back to look over the rail again.

Again, she felt someone's eyes on her.

She whirled around. This time, she glimpsed a face in one of the portholes.

Billy.

Smiling at her.

Taunting her.

Linda rushed inside, hoping to catch Billy as he left the stateroom. But when she came through a door at one end of the hallway, the door at the other end was just swinging shut.

Linda opened every door she could find and searched every hallway and corridor, from one end of the ship to the other. Part of her was afraid, but the part of her that was fuming mad inside made her keep looking. Billy was on this boat, and Linda had every intention of finding him.

The hours passed. The ship fell silent. Soon, the only people awake were Linda and Billy. Chasing each other. Hunting each other down.

She remembered the horoscope she'd read just that morning: *Events bring you closer to your goal. The end is within reach.*

At some point, Billy would show himself. He was like that. Because Billy had a goal, too.

Killing Linda.

She climbed to the highest deck, the one that gave her the best view of the rest of the ship. Overhead, stars twinkled in the sky. The moon was full and thin strands of misty gray clouds blew across it. Linda filled her lungs with sea air.

Billy was always able to read her mind. And so she whispered to him, "I'm ready."

From the very tip of the boat, a voice called out to her, "Over here, Linda."

Linda looked out across the decks. Down below, on the entertainment deck, a mast flew from the prow of the boat. A figure clung to the very top of that mast.

Billy.

"You want your Libra?" he shouted out to her. "Come and get him."

Linda raced down to the lower deck and across the wide, wooden expanse at its tip. The night she'd met Billy, he had kissed her—in this very spot.

Billy was thirty feet up on the mast, clinging to the pole. "Hurry, Linda," he cried into the wind. "You wouldn't want me to fall, would you?"

The skirt of her dress whipped around Linda's legs as she started to climb. She gathered it up and tied it around her waist, leaving her movements free. Hand over hand, she went up the ladder that led to the top of the mast. She kept her eyes trained on Billy. One false move from him, and they could both get seriously hurt.

At the top of the mast, there was a small platform. Billy stood there, a huge grin on his face. "I thought this would be the most romantic spot," he said.

"For what?" Linda asked.

"For my proposal. Will you marry me, Linda?"

Linda didn't know whether to laugh or scream. Billy had lost his mind.

Then she remembered...

Control a Libra's heart and you've controlled his soul.

"Sure, Billy," she said. "Sure, I'll marry you."

Linda overcame all her fear and all her disgust and actually took Billy's hands in hers. He helped her up to the platform. Now she was face-to-face with her enemy. The wind whipped around them. The sea rushed by below.

"I'll agree to marry you if you come down the mast with me and admit to everyone what you've done," she said, thinking on her feet. "I need you, Billy. I need you to back me up."

Billy smiled. For a long time, Linda held her breath. She could see him thinking, she could see his green eyes pondering what she'd said. Would he go along with it?

Then the smile dropped from his face. Billy's hands gripped Linda's waist. His eyes, when he looked up at her, were cold and hard.

Linda froze. She had her answer.

"Back you up?" Billy echoed. His voice chilled her to the bone. "I don't think so. No, Linda, there's really only one way to end this, now that I think about it. Marriage would be nice, but I think we should do something more *dramatic*, don't you?"

Billy loomed over her. His hands around her waist tightened even more.

For the first time, Linda was scared to death.

"What do you mean?" she asked.

But Billy wouldn't answer. Instead, he stepped to the edge of the platform. The deck of the ship was tiny, and very far away. Instead, what Linda noticed was the sea—cold, dark, raging waters. Billy's arm was firmly around her waist as he pulled her to the edge of the platform.

Linda squirmed, trying to free herself.

"Stop," she said. "Let go of me."

But Billy only laughed. "Not on your life, Linda!"

With that, he leapt from the platform, pulling Linda right along with him.

CHAPTER 18

Linda plunged into the dark sea.

She fought against the current dragging her down. Her lungs were bursting for air, but she held on. Frantically, she clawed her way to the surface. When she finally burst through to the air, she was hundreds of feet away from the ship, and Billy was nowhere in sight.

She pushed the wet hair out of her eyes. Her long dress clung to her legs. As much as she hated to do it, Linda ripped the skirt from the dress, sacrificing it to the ocean. There was no way she could swim with it dragging her down.

Linda had taken two strokes when she heard Billy calling out behind her.

"Don't leave me here, Linda," he said. "You know I'm a bad swimmer."

"You should have thought of that before you

threw us both off the mast," Linda shouted back.

"Linda, please. I'm going to die out here."

Linda kept swimming.

"Linda! Help!"

She took a few more strokes. Billy started to yell and scream and splash in the water, but still she didn't turn around. It took all her strength not to listen to him. She focused on the boat and the thought of rescue.

Billy was on his own.

"You're going to regret this, Linda," said Billy. She heard him flailing in the water. "Especially since there's a couple of sharks out here."

"Very funny," Linda cried over her shoulder.

"I'm telling you the truth," Billy yelled. "One of them's circling me. The other's swimming right toward you. I can see him."

Linda dared herself not to look. It was just another one of Billy's stupid tricks, and she wasn't going to fall for it.

"Nine o'clock high, Linda," Billy cried. "Twenty feet to your left."

Don't listen to him, she told herself. *He's lying.*

Then she saw the fin for herself.

Cutting through the waves, two tiny, evil shadows in the night.

"Don't panic," Billy warned. "I've heard they

can smell fear. I'm serious."

One shark was getting closer, bearing down on Linda.

Panic raced through her.

There was a shark in the water, and it was swimming right toward her.

Linda froze.

Then she had an idea. She remembered reading somewhere that you could knock out a shark by punching it in the nose. She almost laughed, hysterical. It sounded like a ridiculous idea. Who wanted to get close enough to a shark to actually punch it?

But she was running out of ideas.

Linda stopped swimming and waited for the shark to come closer. She treaded water. Her whole body tensed. The shark cut through the water, heading straight for her.

Soon it was so close, Linda could actually see its awful teeth.

Just as the shark was about to take a whopping bite out of her, Linda punched it—hard—right in the nose.

The shark's wail cut through the night. The fish flopped over, unconscious, disappearing into the sea.

"What's going on over there?" Billy cried.

"I knocked it out!" Linda shouted back.

"Well, get over here and knock mine out, too!" Billy begged.

The adrenaline was coursing through her. In five swift crawl strokes, she had gotten close enough to see Billy. But the other shark was circling him now. Linda couldn't save Billy without encountering the shark.

"Do something!" Billy begged. Even in the dark, Linda could see the fear in his eyes. "He's going to kill me!"

The shark stopped circling—and zeroed in. It charged. Billy let out a long wail. Linda froze. She had to do something! But what?

"Help!" Billy cried.

Linda watched in horror as Billy shot up high in the air. Then the shark sucked him down into the dark waters, and Billy disappeared.

Billy's cries echoed in Linda's ears the whole way back to the boat. She could still hear them long after she was pulled back onboard.

Linda was in shock.

At least, that's what they told her.

"It's understandable," said Carol. "What you went through was awful."

Billy was dead.

The shark had killed him.

She'd seen it with her very own eyes. The shark dragged Billy down into the ocean, and Linda had swum away.

She was free.

Or was she?

They took her to Captain Jim's stateroom. They bundled her in a towel and put a cup of hot chocolate in her hand. Someone had given it to her, but she didn't remember who, or what it tasted like. Instead, she replayed the scene with Billy and the shark.

Over and over.

Billy was dead.

Linda had left him there.

The shark had killed him.

"Linda, what's wrong?" Carol asked. "You don't feel guilty, do you? There was nothing you could have done."

"What if he's still alive?" Linda asked.

"That's ridiculous," Jim said. "There's no way Billy could have survived the shark attack."

"I know," said Linda. Her whole body felt numb. "It's just that…if Billy survived, he'll never forgive me for leaving him there. I just left him! I left him, and I know he's going to come back and make me pay."

She knew it sounded crazy, but she couldn't stop thinking about the last look Billy had given her, right before the shark dragged him down.

It wasn't surprise.

It was anger.

Anger that Linda hadn't done anything to save his life.

"Linda, listen to you!" Carol exclaimed. "It was you or Billy out there. You saved yourself. What else could you have done?"

Linda started to cry. "Oh, Carol, it's just so awful. I wanted to get rid of Billy, but not like this. This was horrible."

Carol put her arm around Linda. "Believe me, Linda, someday you'll be able to forget all this. Someday, Billy will just be a bad memory. Right now, you need to relax and get some rest. Why don't you go back to our cabin and have a nice hot bath? I'll come by in a few minutes to make sure you're okay. All right?"

"Sure." Linda nodded. Just listening to Carol's soft, warm voice was reassuring. "You think I'll be able to forget about this, honestly?"

"I'm sure you will," Carol said.

"There's no way Billy could have survived the shark attack. He's dead, Linda. Dead."

The words echoed in Linda's ears as she stumbled back to her cabin. Maybe her cousin was right. Maybe a hot bath would take her mind off this terrible night. A long, long soak, long enough to forget Billy Jackson—forever.

About ten feet from her cabin door, Linda noticed the bloody spot on the carpet. No, not a spot, Linda thought. A trail.

A bloody trail.

She started to tremble.

No! a voice screamed inside her head. *It can't be! I saw the shark! I saw it grab Billy! He's dead,* she told herself, *just like Carol said.*

But the trail of blood didn't lie. And the trail of blood could only mean one thing...

Billy Jackson was alive.

The door flung open. Billy stood there, his face a pulpy mess. Blood dripped into his eyes from a wound on his forehead. His lips were cut and swollen, and he had deep gashes on his neck and arms. His clothes hung from his body in shreds. At his feet was a mangled...thing. At first, Linda couldn't tell what it was. But then she realized. The shark.

"That's right, Linda," Billy managed to say. An awful smile spread across his blood-soaked face. "I beat the shark—and I'll beat you, too."

CHAPTER 19

It wasn't possible.

Billy couldn't be alive.

But he was.

Her nightmare would never end.

Linda shrieked as Billy hurled the shark carcass at her. The shark knocked Linda sideways. She fell to the ground, and Billy loomed over her.

"You ruined everything," he said contemptuously. "You couldn't love me back. You had to doubt me. They always doubt me, and—see? It always ends like this."

Linda kicked the shark off her, gagging at the smell of it. "What do you mean, always?" she asked.

"Never mind." Billy grabbed Linda by the arm and yanked her to her feet. "It doesn't matter."

Linda struggled to free herself from Billy's

grasp, but he just held on tighter. He dragged her, squirming in his arms, toward the stairs.

"Where are we going?" Linda asked. "Where are you taking me?"

"Oh, Linda, you always did ask too many questions," Billy said. "Don't you remember what curiosity did to the cat?"

Billy forced Linda down the stairs. Then he pushed her along a maze of corridors until they came to the door Billy had first showed Linda on the tour he'd given her, way back at the beginning of the cruise.

He opened the door and shoved Linda through. Then he wrapped an arm tightly around her waist and dragged her down the dark hallways. Around her, Linda could hear the sound of the ship's engines chugging away. Tomorrow morning, the sun would be shining in Fort Lauderdale.

Would Linda make it to tomorrow?

If Billy had his way, probably not.

The deeper into the ship they went, the more certain Linda became.

Billy was going to kill her this time.

For real.

She wished Carol and Captain Jim a long and happy life together.

At the very end of the boat, Billy stood Linda

before the last—and largest—hatch. He held her tightly to him while he opened the hatch. When he threw it open, Linda saw for herself the white surf and the churning waves.

"A watery grave, Linda," said Billy with an evil smile. "And it's all yours."

"Billy, no!" Linda was in a deep panic by now. "Think about what you're doing. It doesn't have to be this way."

"That's what they all say," Billy announced. "But they're always wrong. It comes down to this, Linda. You said you were going to love me, and you didn't. Before, when we were on the mast, I thought that meant we should die together. But then you left me with the sharks and I changed my mind. I don't deserve to die. But you do."

"I'm sorry." Linda's voice came out a wail. "I didn't know what else to do."

"Sure, Linda, sure." Billy's voice was cold and distant. "There's all sorts of reasons for what you did. But they don't change what I'm going to do to you."

Billy pulled a length of rope from his pocket.

"Recognize this?" he asked.

Linda swallowed in fear.

It was the same rope she'd used to tie Billy to his chair, earlier that evening.

Only that evening.

It felt like days since she and Billy had been in her cabin.

"I'm glad I saved it," Billy said sarcastically.

Billy hauled Linda over to one of the hatches. He tied her hands behind her back, then looped the rope through the hatch's metal handle. After that, he ran the rope down to her ankles and tied them together, too.

"What did you mean about the others?" Linda asked, hoping to distract Billy. "You said 'they're' always wrong. Who?"

Billy narrowed his eyes at Linda. "Never mind. It's not important."

He grabbed a long wooden board that was leaning against the wall. Then he picked up a monkey wrench.

"I want you to tell me, Billy," Linda pleaded. "Because I was thinking, we never really got to know one another that well. Maybe that was the problem. We were strangers, then it got really intense really fast, and then we were breaking up. Maybe if we tried again. More slowly this time, you know. If you talk to me, then I'll bet you anything we can work it out."

While Linda was babbling, Billy was busy with the wood and the monkey wrench. The board had two holes drilled in one end of it. Linda watched as Billy set the board down, lining up the holes with two bolts in the floor. Just watching him, Linda felt a chill spread over her. Billy had done a lot of planning. The holes in the board matched the bolts perfectly. When Billy was done, the board stuck out the end of the open hatch. Just like a—

"A plank," Billy announced, looking up at her with a smile. "Exactly. You're going to walk the plank, Linda. You know I wanted to be the captain of this ship. And that's what any true captain would do, if he had a first mate who left him to the sharks. Make you walk the plank—for all your treachery and disloyalty."

"Billy!" Linda's voice was hoarse and desperate. "How can you do this? Tommy was an accident. I know that now. But how can you kill me like this—in cold blood?"

"You think you're the first, don't you?" Billy said. "You think you're the first one I've hurt like this? Well, maybe I've never taken it quite this far, but all along you've been able to make me lose my head, go farther. I guess that's just your special talent, Linda. I feel more for you than I've felt for any of the others."

Now Linda was really freaked out. Billy must be talking about his other girlfriends. That's who "they" were. The other girls he dated, the ones Justine was telling her about. The ones he hurt so bad that they were never the same.

"So I'm the last in a long line?" Linda asked, braving the question. "You go around hurting girls, is that it, Billy? And now you're going to start killing them, too? When will it end? You're sick, Billy, you know that? You need help."

"Spoken like a true Capricorn," came a woman's voice, soft and low. "Trying every tactic—right to the very end."

Linda looked into the darkened recesses of the platform. "Who's there?" she asked.

"Billy knows," the voice said. "Why don't you ask him?"

Billy's face relaxed into a grin. "My reinforcements have arrived!" he cried. "What took you so long?"

Linda's heart started to pound and she realized just how trapped she was. All along, Billy had known he'd need help. Help to get him back on the boat, but also help in following her. Suddenly, Linda thought about all the times she'd run into trouble. In the sauna. At the pool. Someone had known, each of those times, where she'd been.

Billy had never been working alone.

But who was it? Who was his ally?

"Why don't you guess, Linda?" Billy asked, reading her mind yet again.

"Why don't you tell her?" the voice replied.

"Why don't you just show your face," Linda snapped, "and stop playing these games."

Linda held her breath.

It had to be Marla. Tough, smooth-talking Marla. Marla had not wanted her to turn Billy in. What had she said? *Relax, Linda. Why ruin a good thing?*

"Come on," Billy said. "Let's stop messing around."

"Billy's right, Marla. It's time to show your face."

"Marla?" Billy looked at Linda in surprise. "What makes you think it's Marla?"

The figure stepped from the shadows. "Hello, Billy, hello, Linda," she said.

It wasn't Marla at all.

It was Justine.

CHAPTER 20

"Linda, you look shocked," Justine said with a small smile. "What's the matter? Cat got your tongue?"

Billy put an arm around Justine's shoulders and kissed her lightly on the cheek.

Justine accepted Billy's kiss with a smile.

Suddenly, Linda remembered the note slipped under her door. "There are two sides to every Libra," it had said. Had Justine been trying to hint to Linda even then about Billy? Linda shook her head, still trying to clear her thoughts. Justine even looked different tonight. Instead of her usual slumped shoulders and the scowl she'd worn ever since Tommy's death, the girl was smiling and laughing—even wearing makeup and a ring.

Linda's gaze settled on the familiar piece of jewelry.

Not just any ring, she thought. *My ring.*

The one Billy had given to her.

Justine caught Linda's eye. "What did you think, that I'd let a perfectly good piece of jewelry go to waste?"

"Did Billy give you that?" Linda asked.

"He didn't have to," Justine replied. "I took it for myself."

Linda was sure Billy would be upset to see that Justine was wearing the ring he'd bought for Linda. Instead, he took one look at the ring and said, "I never gave you enough credit, J. Maybe we shouldn't have broken up after all."

"That wasn't my choice, Billy," Justine replied. "Remember?"

"Once we get rid of Linda," Billy said, "why don't we give it another try?"

He put an arm around Justine's waist and drew her close. Justine's smile widened.

Linda thought she was going to be sick. She couldn't believe she had to watch this!

Justine stroked Billy's chest. "But you broke my heart. How do I know you won't drop me again? Besides, isn't Linda more your type?"

"I thought so," Billy said. "I guess I was wrong."

Justine looked at Linda over Billy's shoulder.

"You see, Linda? That's why you should never love a Libra. They don't know what they want! Let me tell you a little story.

"Once upon a time, Billy and I were in love. Then he got weird. Really weird. All my friends had warned me about him. They said he'd acted strange with other girls. Compulsive, obsessive. I didn't believe them until I saw it for myself."

Billy hung his head. "I said I was sorry." He shrugged. "You know how I can get sometimes."

"I sure do. And now Linda does, too." Justine went on. "So I took a cruise. To get Billy out of my system, maybe even meet another guy. And guess what? Billy shows up. On the *same* cruise!" Justine laughed. "Who would have believed it? Talk about a coincidence. And of course, you fell madly in love with Linda. And of course, I was ready to tell her a million times what trouble you were."

"So *you* were the one who left me the note," Linda guessed.

"That's right," Justine admitted. "I was going to tell you more, but then I started hanging out with Tommy, and I let it go. I guess I hoped that when Billy showed you his real self, you'd see it was a mistake. Besides, I was in love with Tommy. I was in love with him, Billy, and you killed him— just like that. I hate you!"

"If you hate Billy, why did you let him back on the boat?" Linda asked. "Why didn't you tell anyone what Marla and Kevin had done?"

Justine sighed. "Marla and Kevin thought it would be fun to watch you and Billy go at each other. They didn't know how dangerous he was. I was going to turn him in, but then I realized the possibilities."

"Of what?" Linda didn't like the glassy look she saw in Justine's eyes. The girl had lost it.

"Revenge," Justine said, drawing out the word. "It doesn't come often to Sagittarians. But when it does, it sure feels sweet. I plan to get rid of you, Billy Jackson—forever."

CHAPTER 21

Justine wrestled the monkey wrench out of Billy's hand. Before Billy could defend himself, Justine brought it down on his head, hard.

Billy raised a hand to defend himself.

Too late.

He let out a small cry as the wrench made contact with his skull. Then he slumped to the ground, unconscious.

"Looks like Billy already had a little trip planned for you," she said. "Now you're both going to take it."

"Both of us?" Linda asked.

"Unfortunately for you, Linda, you're a witness." She shrugged, displaying her Sagittarian matter-of-factness. "So first you're going to help me with Billy, and then I'm going to send you over, too."

"You won't get away with it," Linda said. She kept her eyes open, ready for Justine to make a false move, ready to take her chance when it happened. "They'll know what you did. My cousin will, and so will Captain Jim."

Justine kept the monkey wrench poised in one hand while she untied Linda with the other.

"Fat chance," she said. "You'll be gone, Linda. They won't even find your body. Or Billy's. It'll look like some crazy plan of Billy's, gone bad. No one will even know I was down here. It's the end, Linda."

Justine's plan *was* the end.

Unless—somehow—Linda found a way to stop her.

By now, Justine had untied Linda's hands. "Do your feet," she ordered.

While Linda was bending over, she saw her chance.

And she took it.

She grabbed Justine by the waist and tackled her to the ground. They landed right next to Billy. For a moment, Linda had the upper hand. Justine was pinned under her, squirming.

Linda forced Justine's arms over her head. Justine held the monkey wrench inches away from Linda's grasp. She was that close. From below,

Justine gazed at Linda, a questioning look in her dark brown eyes.

"Go for it, Linda," she said. "What's stopping you?"

Linda thought for a second.

It was a second too long.

Justine swung Linda off her. Once she was kneeling and Linda was on the floor next to her, she raised the monkey wrench, threatening Linda with it.

"One more move like that," she warned, "and you're going to have a serious head wound. Think about it!"

By now, Billy was coming around. Since he could barely stand, Justine got Linda to help him to his feet. With Billy in the lead and Linda right behind him, Justine shoved them both toward the plank.

At the very edge of the ship, Linda made the mistake of taking a look down. Sea spray churned upward, and violent waves rocked the boat. She could see the boat's propeller, ugly metal blades splitting the ocean apart.

If she fell onto the blades, it was all over.

But if she jumped away from them, would she really be able to survive?

In front of her, Billy fell to his knees.

Instinctively, Linda reached out to save him from falling into the ocean. Behind her, Justine laughed.

"You think there's hope for you?" she taunted. "You should have let him fall just now. Then he wouldn't have to face the end of the plank. Once you get out to the edge, there's no turning back."

Linda couldn't believe the icy tone in Justine's voice. Gone was her fun-loving Sagittarian friend. With the dark ocean below her, and Justine pushing her toward the end of the plank, Linda gave up hope.

She was going to die.

There was no way around it.

At the edge of the plank, Justine ordered Billy to his knees.

"How does it feel?" she shouted above the roar of the ocean. "How does it feel to know you're going to die?"

Billy was still dazed. His eyes rolled back in his head and his body swayed in the wind. Justine reached past Linda, gave her a small smile, and shoved Billy over.

Linda gasped. Right before he fell, Billy's eyes snapped open in amazement. Then he reached out, his arms flailing.

At the very last moment Billy managed the impossible—he grabbed onto the plank and saved himself—just barely—from drowning.

Linda watched the whole thing as if it were happening in slow motion. Justine's shove. Billy's horrified expression. Billy hanging from the plank, his feet dangling in the air, his desperate cries louder than the ocean's roar beneath him.

"Help!" he shouted. "Don't do this to me!"

But Justine just laughed. She shot her leg around Linda and stomped on Billy's fingers.

"Stop it!" Linda cried.

She pushed Justine away from Billy. The girl fell backward, almost losing her balance, almost disappearing over the edge. But not quite.

On her right, Billy was crying out for help. On her left, Justine was heading toward her, ready for another round. Linda braced herself. The wind made it hard to keep her balance, but she crouched down to keep herself from falling. Then she reached out for Billy's hand.

"Hold on!" she shouted. "I'll pull you up."

"You're going to save him?" Justine asked in disbelief. "Why?"

"Because this game has gone on way too long," Linda told her. "Billy deserves to be punished, but he doesn't deserve to die."

"That's where we disagree," Justine said.

Linda yanked on Billy's arm, pulling him

halfway to safety. But before she could haul him onto the plank, Justine threw herself at both of them.

"Let go of him!" she shouted.

Linda fended her off with one arm, trying to hold on to Billy with the other. The hand that gripped Billy's felt as if it was coming out of its socket. But still she held on.

"Let him go, I said!"

Justine tried to push Linda away from Billy. But Linda was ready for her this time. She lashed out at Justine, catching her in the stomach with the blow.

Justine teetered sideways. Her arms flailed, and she went flying backward. She grabbed for the plank. Her fingertips grazed the board—and missed.

By inches.

The last thing Linda saw was the look of horror in Justine's warm brown eyes.

And then Justine was gone, plunging into the water below. She heard the ocean swallow her. She held her breath and waited for Justine to resurface.

But she never did.

The boat plowed on, and soon Linda couldn't even find the spot where Justine had disappeared.

And somehow, through the whole thing,

Linda managed to cling to Billy's hand.

Only seconds had passed. Seconds that felt like hours.

Linda turned her attention to Billy now. She reached with both hands to pull Billy to safety. He was still dazed from Justine's blow and nearly unconscious from the effort of hanging on. This time, Linda knew Billy wouldn't harm her.

Even a Libra had to give up *sometime*.

Once she had him all the way up on the plank, Linda stared at his prone figure, amazed that it was really over.

Billy was captured.

She was victorious.

Her nightmare had ended—at last.

And yet, even defeated, Billy Jackson had to have the last word.

"Leave it to a Capricorn to do the right thing," he said, his eyelids fluttering open just an inch. "You should have let me die, Linda. Don't you know you'll live to regret it?"

Check your horoscope for January—
Zodiac Chiller #6 is on its way!

Jenna had better watch out, or she'll be the next...

PISCES DROWNING

"What are you doing here?" Jenna asked.

"I broke out of the detention center," Nicky admitted. "I couldn't take it anymore. I couldn't stand being separated from you."

Jenna felt a wave of dizziness sweep over her as the meaning of Nicky's words sank in. "You escaped," she said slowly. "They're going to be looking for you. And when they find you, it's going to be worse. Oh, Nicky, why—"

"Shhh." Nicky silenced her with a kiss. "Don't worry. They're not going to find me. I've got a plan. But what I need right now is to be able to hide out for a while. And that part is easy."

"It is?"

"I'm going to hide right here. In your room."

"Are you crazy?" Jenna almost shrieked. "My

father is a cop. The man who arrested you, in case you've forgotten."

"Which is why this is the perfect hideout," Nicky said smoothly. "The last place anyone would look for me is inside Detective William Durrell's house."

VICKI KAMIDA

Vicki Kamida is a double Cancer—sun sign and rising sign—which makes her a mystery to herself and others. She lives in Pasadena, California, with her husband—a very compatible Pisces. And like most Cancers, she loves her home, friends, and a good meal. She is the author of nearly two dozen books for younger readers, and she also teaches writing to college students and adults. Because her moon is in Gemini, she likes to talk almost as much as she likes to write.